Ugly Sweater Christmas

The Holidays with You

Shannon O'Connor

Ugly Sweater Christmas

SHANNON O'CONNOR

Copyright © 2024 Shannon O'Connor
All rights reserved.

All rights reserved. No part of this publication may be reproduced, distributed, or transmitted in any form or by any means, except in the case of brief quotations embodied in critical reviews and articles.

Any resemblance to persons alive or dead is purely coincidental.

Cover by *Alt19 Creative*.

Formatted by Shannon O'Connor.

Edited by Victoria Ellis of *Cruel Ink Publishing*.

❦ Created with Vellum

Emma's Holiday To Do List

1. Go Job Hunting & Christmas Shopping
2. Warm up with hot cocoa in Bryant Park
3. See the tree at Rockefeller Center
4. Mail a letter to Santa at Macy's
5. Cozy up In an igloo at 230 fifth
6. Grab coffee at Ralph's
7. Sak's 5th ave light show
8. Christmas lights at Hudson yards
9. Miracle on 9th street
10. dinner at Oscar Wilde
11. Go sledding in Central Park
12. See New York Botanical Garden's Train Show and Christmas Lights

Chapter 1

Jess

Do you ever have one of those days where everything seems to be falling apart? Don't fucking ask me if that's me. It all started with my life falling apart one December morning.

I walk into my office at the Library and instantly know something is off. It's almost like the entire vibe of the office is off. I place my bag on my chair, and I notice my coworker, Ann, isn't here yet. It's weird because out of the two of us she's always here early, if not at least on time. Meanwhile, I'm usually five minutes late. It's something I'm working on, but honestly, who cares if I'm perpetually five little minutes late? I always stay five minutes extra to make up for it.

Ann's bag isn't here and neither is her coffee—it's something I realize right away because the aroma always fills the office. I furrow my brows and decide to grab a cup of coffee from the kitchen. It's a small room that has the essentials for the office, and I make a dark coffee from the Keurig machine, watching as it fills my *In my reading era* mug that my best friend, Emma, recently gave me. Emma is one of those friends that love giving random gifts. She says it's her love language, but I think she just likes shopping and can pass it off as gift giving if she grabs things for other people while she's shopping for herself.

"Jess? Do you have a moment?" My boss pops his head into the kitchen, and I nod, smiling.

"Sure, what's up?"

"Can we talk in my office?" he asks. I probably would worry if this wasn't a weekly occurrence. He likes to have conversations in his office because it's more private and there's less of a chance of anyone overhearing. Not that we were talking about anything confidential most of the time.

"Sure." I stop and grab my coffee, blowing on it as I walk into his office.

"Have a seat." He gestures to the chair in front of his desk as he sits down.

I place my coffee on his desk and take a seat.

"I'm afraid we're going to have to let you go."

"W--what?" My jaw drops open.

"I'm sorry, we have a ton of budget cuts this quarter, and I have to make cuts where I can. I hate this. You're an incredible employee, and I'd love to write you a glowing recommendation letter, but we have to let you go. You're fired," he says, sighing.

"I-I'm fired?" I repeat the words he says because they're so unbelievable that I can't fully decipher them.

"I'm afraid so, yes."

"I just don't understand." Tears fall from my eyes; it's new for me because I'm not a crier.

"I'm sorry, it's purely a financial decision. You're not the only one I've had to let go today." He frowns.

"Ana? Is that why she wasn't here?" I ask.

"I'm afraid I can't discuss that with you." he says quietly.

"I just, is there anything I can do?"

"No. I'm sorry, I'm afraid you have to pack up your stuff and be out of the office by the end of the day."

"O-okay." I've worked here for over five years, and suddenly my career was over in the blink of an eye.

I stand to leave when my boss calls my name, and I'm so desperate for him to change his mind that I look back, wide-eyed and hopeful.

"You left your coffee," he says quietly. My face falls, and I nod.

"Thanks." I didn't want to leave the mug behind.

I head to my office and find an empty file box to put my stuff in. I don't have much, just photos of me and my girlfriend, Camille. A few photos of me and my best friend, Emma, and some knickknacks I like keeping on my desk. They're mostly reading-based things that Emma's given me over the years. I pile them into the box, and I notice Ana's desk has been cleared off, too. I wish she had said goodbye but I'm sure she was just as upset as I am.

I pack all my things into the box and sigh as I make my way out of the office. It feels like I'm doing the walk of shame. Not that I've ever actually done one of those, but this is definitely the lowest I've ever felt.

I decide to take the subway home. I know I should be trying to save money rather than Ubering all the way to Brooklyn. Plus, no one on the subway cares if you're crying. Everyone is on their morning commute, and I'm on my way home from being fired. I probably look homeless and dumped. But thankfully, I'll be going home to Camille and getting some comfort from her. She works from home most days, and she'll be home today. I'm looking forward to the cuddles and comfort from her. Knowing I'll see my girlfriend soon is the only thing that makes me relax on the way home from my ex-job.

When I get to the apartment, I get out my key, almost dropping my walk of shame box on the sidewalk. Out crashes a framed photo of Camille and me. I frown, picking it up and leaving behind the broken glass. I place it back in the box and make a mental note to fix that later and call maintenance to get rid of the glass.

"Camille! I'm home!" I call out as I walk through the door. Placing the box on the living room table, I slide off my shoes and make a beeline for Camille's office.

"Babe?" I call again. Maybe she went out while I was gone. I should've texted her when I was on my way back but I was just too upset to type out what had happened.

"Hey boy," I bend down to pet our dog, Duke. He wags his tail, and I smile at him. At least he's here to greet me.

"Oh! Right there!" I hear a breathy voice call out. *Camille?* I smile to myself. My girlfriend is having some solo play time—

"Harder!" I hear another voice say and my jaw clenches, stopping my thoughts and turning my body into an inferno.

"Oh my fucking god." I snap open the door and find Camille, head deep between the thighs of a naked woman that is not me. My jaw drops as they both look at me like deer in headlights.

I slam the door shut and ignore the calls for me to come back. This cannot be happening. I pinch myself; this has to be some sort of a bad dream. I mean what the hell did I do to deserve a day like today? Was I some mass murderer in my past life, and this is how I'm paying for it?

"Jess," Camille says running out of the room with just a sheet on.

"Please tell me this is some kind of a joke, and I didn't just catch you fucking some other woman in our bed." I growl.

"You weren't supposed to be home." She says the words as if that suddenly makes it better. Like it was my fault I came home early.

"Oh, my fucking bad, please CONTINUE." I roll my eyes.

"I just mean, I didn't want you to find out this way." She sighs.

"What do you mean?"

"I mean, look, Crystal is my girlfriend. We've been seeing each other for a little while now. It isn't some fling. This isn't some random woman. I just didn't know how to tell you."

I stare at her like she's nuts. Because she fucking has to be to be telling me this right now. I have the urge to pinch myself again. This can't be fucking happening.

"I don't understand." I stop the tears from falling because she doesn't deserve to see me cry. Not like this.

"I didn't know how to tell you, but now that it's out... well. My name is on the lease and Crystal and I are going to be living together. I need you to move out," she says quietly, like she isn't altering my life out of the fucking blue.

"I'm sorry, I don't think I heard you correctly. You cheated on *me* and you want *me* to move out?"

"Well, yeah. My name *is* on the lease after all."

"Because you said it's a pain in the ass to change! Not so you can move your girlfriend in!" I exclaim.

"Well, yeah." She just shrugs. Like she isn't the one in the wrong here. Like I didn't just find her tongue deep in another woman.

"Un-fucking-believable." I scoff.

"You can come back another day and get your stuff. Maybe when Crystal isn't here."

"Where the hell am I supposed to go now?"

"That really isn't my problem anymore." She shrugs. I hate how nonchalant she's being. Like I was just some fling to her, like we weren't together for three years.

I grab my sad little box of things and leave the apartment I've known for the last few years without a piece of clothing besides what I have on my back. I sit on the steps of my—well, Camille's—apartment and try to gather my thoughts. Where the hell am I going to go?

Chapter 2

Emma

"Can I buy you a drink?" a blond man at the bar asks.

"No, thank you." I shake my head with a kind smile. His head falls, and he walks away in defeat.

"That's the third one in ten minutes; this has to be some kind of a record," Ellie points out.

"I don't think so, it's just men being men. It's not like any women have come up to us." I sigh.

"Don't speak too soon," Ellie mumbles, but before I can ask what she means, a woman with bleach blonde hair walks up to us.

"Hey, I noticed you turned down my friends, and I'm hoping it's because you're into women. Would I be able to get your number?" she asks with a clean smile.

"It is, but why don't you tell me your name before you get my number?" I counter.

"Terran, but everyone calls me Tee." She tosses her blonde hair over her shoulder.

"It's lovely to meet you. Why don't you give me your number, and I'll give you a call tonight?" I suggest. I like being the one with the power when it comes to giving out numbers. I don't want to be waiting around for a call or a text to come through.

"Sounds good." I hand her my phone, and she adds in her number then hands it back to me.

"I look forward to a text." She winks and heads back to her friends with a smug look on her face.

"Wow, are you actually going to call her?"

"Probably not, but it got men to stop coming over here and trying which is something." I laugh.

"That's true." Ellie smirks.

"I have a date tonight with Hellen, the one from the mail room, anyway. I'm sure I'll score with her; our texts have been spicy as hell."

"Ah, the single life," she teases. She's been in a committed long-term relationship for as long as I've known her.

"Do you ever miss it?" I ask, but I already know her answer.

"Nope, I wouldn't change a thing. I love Reese." She smiles proudly.

"Good, I don't need you two breaking up and being my competition when we're out and about together," I tease.

"Now, you against Reese with the ladies is something I'd definitely like to see." She laughs.

"Well, we should head back to work," I suggest and Ellie nods.

We both worked at New Chic designs. It's a fashion company where we create the designs for lines of clothing. I work on models of all size ranges, and I do mean all. Like from a ooo to a 6xl+. Ellie works specifically on plus-size clothing for her lines. We have a great work environment, but according to Ellie, it hasn't always been this way. She used to have a terrible boss and no fun co-workers. I definitely got a job there at the right time. But things have always had a way of working out for me. I got the job right out of college, and I've been working there for the last two years full time. I'll probably keep working here until I start my own line someday. It's a great way to learn the industry and meet the people you need to know to be successful.

"I'll see you later." Ellie smiles and heads into her office, and I do the same.

I'm working on the winter 2024 line for the company, and that means I need to think all things festive and bright. It's no trouble to do since I love Christmas. The winter isn't my favorite, but the holidays sure are. I'm designing a lot of reds and blacks, which happen to be two of my favorite colors. I'm currently working on a red tech coat that's thermal inside and has the cutest cinched waist. It'll look good no matter what size someone is, and that's so important to me.

I'm working on the mannequin for a while, and when I finally finish I'm grateful to kick off my heels under my desk and draw up some new designs. It's almost five p.m. when I look at the clock again, and I realize it's time to head home. I'm someone who would like to leave work at the office, but also someone who can't possibly do that, so I grab my iPad and slip it into my purse. I often get hit with a stroke of genius on the train or in the shower, and I just need to be able to get my idea down. Besides, it isn't like I'm paid to only have ideas at work. I make enough money that I can afford to take things home.

I go home alone, and think about the girl from the bar today. I should probably text her but I know I probably wouldn't. It's unlikely she'll hear from me again, and I like it that way. I'm looking forward to hooking up with Hellen and calling it a night. After I get home, I'll dress up for my date and go out for some drinks before ending up at one of our places. We'd already talked about it, and neither of us are looking for anything serious so why not have a little fling?

By the time I get home, I shower and shave everything. Thankfully, I'm flexible enough to reach my own ass, and once I'm hairless and moisturized, I get out of the shower. Putting on a fresh face of makeup and curling my blonde locks, I feel more like myself and I'm ready to go out for the night. I walk around my apartment, looking at the view from my living room and soaking it in for a moment. I got this apartment from a couple who was moving out of the city to raise their child upstate in some small town. But damn, I would never give up this view. No matter what. It's amazing no matter what time of day, and right now, as the sun sets over the city, it looks breathtaking.

I look for my shoes and my dress, which I've started keeping in my guest bedroom closet. I had used up most of the space in the closet in my room, and it isn't like anyone else is using this closet, anyway. So I find the right pair of heels that go with the skintight red dress I'm wearing, and I pass by a mirror. I look hot, no wonder I'm going to get laid tonight. I feel sexy and confident. and I am. I have everything I could possibly want and then some. It's like I'm actually blessed. And I don't take it lightly, either. I give back in any way I can. I donate to charities and hold toy drives this time of year. I help out with volunteer work whenever I can, and I'm not one of those rich people who flaunt their money. Besides, my love language is gift giving, so I love giving gifts to those closest to me—and that includes my best friend, Jess.

Speaking of which, I haven't heard from her at all today,

which is very unlike her. We have a habit of texting each other every day, several times a day. Not to check in or anything but just with funny memes or to give quick updates on life. She must've had a busy day for her not to text me at all.

A knock sounds on my door, and I fluff my dress, getting ready to see Hellen on the other side of said door. But when I open the door and see a quiet, sobbing Jess on the other side, I look at her, confused. The moment Jess opens my door with a box in hands and tear-filled eyes, I take her into my arms. She sobs into them for what feels like hours. But I don't say a word, because I know my best friend, and it has to be pretty damn bad for her to be crying like this. So I wait for her to calm down, and when she finally does, I take a deep breath and try to ask her what's wrong.

"I got fired, so I went home, and I found Camille cheating on me." She cries even harder. I know how much that must hurt to say aloud. It's one thing to experience it, but to tell someone about it is a whole other thing.

Chapter 3

Jess

I sob on Emma's couch as she shoots off a quick text, canceling her plans for tonight. I assured her she didn't have to do that, but she convinced me she wants to be here for me. So when she comes back and holds me tight, I try to get myself to stop crying. I'm not the emotional one, that's all Emma. Over the years, she'd been the one to have more heartache and enough drama to last a lifetime. But now she's mainly calmed down in life, and things have been going good for her. I guess that makes me the sappy one in the bunch now. I cry until the tears stop falling, and I finally start to feel a little bit better so I can explain everything in more detail to her.

"So what happened?" she asks quietly.

"Everything is just falling apart. If I didn't need to go home early today then I never would've found out, and I'd still be living a very happy life.

"It's not just that. You know it's not your fault that you went home when you did. Either way, you would've eventually found out. I'm just sorry you had to find them in such a shitty way and on a day when you had so much else going on for you. There's no good time to find something like this out but today sure didn't help anything."

"It's just a lot at once. Like being fired AND finding out about her...it was just like being hit by a car twice in one day. And to find them like that? It's a mental image I'll never get out of my head."

"I understand. I'm sorry you're going through this. is there anything I can do to make this better?"

"Find me a place to live," I joke.

"Well, obviously you're going to stay with me," she says it like it's a basic fact.

"Excuse me?" My brows raise on instinct.

"We've been best friends since middle school, you think we can't live together?" Emma acts as if she's insulted.

"I just. I don't know," I admit. I've never thought about living with Emma before but now it just seems like a plea for help, and I guess it is. I truly am desperate.

"What's not to know? I have an extra bedroom. We just move you in, and I'll get a key made for you in the morning. There's a place on my way to work," she says with a shrug, like getting a key made is the biggest deal here.

"I mean there's still a lot to consider," I point out.

"Like what?" she asks, waiting for my reply but for once, my mind is blank. Maybe she does have a point. I do need somewhere to stay, at least for now. Just until I can get back on my feet. It isn't like I could afford rent now that I'm unemployed.

"Okay, but just until I get back on my feet."

"You can stay as long as you need to." She hugs me, and I smile.

"Thanks." I smile.

"Now, where's your stuff? I know you don't own a lot

but surely everything you have is not in this one box." She narrows her eyes as she looks it over.

"No, I...well—Camille told me to come back another day. So I just left without anything." I sigh.

"That bitch. I'm sorry, I know you might not want to hear that right now, but that's what she is. We're going to get your stuff right after work tomorrow, and she can suck a dick if she has a problem with it," Emma grumbles. She's in full protective beast mode now.

"Okay," I agree, knowing if Emma comes with me I'll be able to get everything without any issue.

I SLEEP like shit in the guest bedroom that Emma makes up for me. It's not due to the bed. I'm just not used to sleeping alone. So when I wake up in the morning to the sound of Emma's alarm, I decide to greet my best friend on her way out to work. She's in the shower while I'm making a cup of coffee, and then I make a second cup for her. I know how she takes it: two sugars and extra cream. Once it's brewed, I look around in her fridge. I mean, she did tell me to make myself at home. And let's be real, we've been best friends for so long that I've already been making myself at home in her space for years now. I find some milk, and then I look for the cereal. I'm halfway through my bowl when Emma comes out of the shower in a fancy, fluffy robe and a pair of slippers.

"I made you some coffee," I say between slurps.

"Thanks, I appreciate that." She smiles and takes the

coffee, pouring it directly into her travel mug. "I just brushed my teeth," she explains and I nod.

"Do you have any plans today?" she asks quietly.

"Nope. Just sit on your couch and cry until you get home," I joke, although it comes out more serious than I intend.

"I'll be home from work early so we can go to your apartment and grab all your stuff. I think I have an old suitcase you can borrow to bring your stuff here in."

"Okay."

"It's in the closet in the guest room, which I'll work on emptying this weekend. It has all my going out clothes in it."

"You don't have to do that. I promise I won't be here that long. It's just until I find another job and get some money coming in," I reassure her.

"And I'm telling you, you can stay as long as you like," she reminds me.

"Well, at least let me pay you rent," I insist.

"Nope." She shakes her blonde head.

"Then how can I repay you?" I frown.

She pauses and thinks for a moment before her eyes light up. "You can come with me to an *Ugly Christmas Sweater Party*."

"Can't I just pay you rent?" I grimace. I'm not the biggest fan of parties, especially right now.

"Nope, it's decided. You'll come to the party with me and have a nice time as your form of repayment." She grins wide.

"Okay." I sigh. There's no arguing with her.

"Yay! Oh, we'll have so much fun! We just have to get you an ugly sweater."

"Why?"

"Because it's an ugly sweater Christmas party. You can't go without an ugly sweater." Her eyes widen as she looks at me like I've lost my brain.

"Oh, of course," I say sarcastically.

"Don't worry, I'll take care of it," she says.

"Okay." I shrug. At least I know she won't put me in something stupid.

"I'll see you after work." She heads to get dressed and then leaves for the day.

I hang out on the couch in Emma's pajamas that she loaned me. I don't cry, but I do wallow in my sadness as I take in my new life. It feels different, losing a job and someone you loved all in the span of twelve hours. Everything feels like it's in shambles, and I'm already over it.

I watch shitty reality television until I hear Emma arrive back home, and then I change into regular clothes. She convinces me to wear something from her closet that makes me look hot, just to make Camille realize what she's missing. I don't feel any better in the outfit, but I'm going to fake it once I get there.

We take the train to Brooklyn with plans of Ubering back to Emma's apartment later. I grab my keys, unlock the front doors, and let myself into the apartment. Thankfully, no one seems to be home. I suppose I could've texted her to be sure of that fact but part of me wishes she was home. Then she could see me moving out and the actual impact that's going to have on her life.

"Let's just grab my stuff and get out of here. I don't want to see her and the new girl together again." I roll my eyes as I think about it.

Emma nods and goes into packing mode. She knows me better than anyone, so she knows my wardrobe and my stuff better than I do. She grabs it, packs it, and we're done within thirty minutes. I don't have a lot of stuff. I'm someone who is more clean and concise with my things. It makes for an easier time to pack and to get things together.

Just as we're about to leave, the front door unlocks and in walks Camille. She looks shocked to see me, and I don't blame her. Maybe I should've given her some kind of a warning. But fuck that. She didn't give me one before she cheated on me. I don't know what to say, and it seems she's just as cautious.

"We're just grabbing Jess's stuff, and then we'll be out of your poorly styled hair," Emma announces. She's always had something to say about Camille's mullet.

"I didn't say she could come over today," Camille says sharply.

"I still had my key," I say pointing to the key on the counter.

"Well, you should've given me some warning." She folds her arms over her chest.

"Like you did when I caught you in bed with some other woman?" I snap.

"That's different—"

"Save it. We're just here to get my things, and then we'll be gone," I repeat. No sense in hashing out the past with her, she won't ever see herself as the bad guy. Even when we dated, she was always the victim in any story she told. Just like I'm sure she'll call her girlfriend and tell this story that way.

"Fine," she grits out and takes a seat on the couch.

"What about Duke?" Emma asks, and I shame myself for not even thinking about Duke. He'd been sleeping when we got here so I didn't think about taking him with us. But I sure as hell won't be leaving him here.

"You can't take him," Camille grumbles.

"Like Hell I can't." Instead of fighting with her, I just begin gathering his things and his food, packing it into boxes.

I move on to the kitchen and start grabbing my mugs. Mugs are probably the things I have the most of. Being a big coffee drinker, I'm also a mug collector. I love different mugs from different places with different sayings. It's one of my favorite things about this apartment—how much cabinet space I had for all my mugs. I'd probably have to keep them in my room at Emma's place. I wrap each one up nicely in the extra box we brought, and just as I am, Camille comes running over.

"That one's mine," she snaps, pointing to a mug that says *New York, New York*.

"I'm pretty positive we got that one together when we first moved in," I remind her. I hadn't meant to take it with me, it was just a habit in grabbing all of the mugs.

"Well, I want it."

I'm about to hand it to her when I have a better idea. I let it slip from my hands and fall crashing into the metal sink. It explodes into countless pieces, and Camille's eyes widen. She looks shocked, and I smirk. I refuse to be nice and walked on. I'm fucking pissed, and she can clean up her own messes now.

"Fuck you," I say with a final wave with Duke under my arm. Emma and I grab my stuff, and we leave the apartment.

I can't help but notice how much better I feel as I leave my old life behind.

Chapter 4

Emma

Jess doesn't complain on the way to the party, which is something I'm grateful for. I know it's not exactly what she wants to be doing today, but I think this party is something she needs. She's been moping around since her life fell apart, not that I blame her. But I think she needs a change of pace just to get her out of her slump. We walk the three blocks over from our apartment to Ellie's, which is coincidentally close.

The snow is falling, and the brownstones are each decorated for Christmas already. It makes it look like something out of a Hallmark movie...if Hallmark movies were ever set in New York City. I don't watch a lot of those movies because they rarely ever have two female leads. Wreaths, blow up Santas, and lots of snow falling over the steps of each house make me feel like I'm in a true winter wonderland. I walk by in awe, my gloved hands in my pockets, still too chilly from the temperature drop. I'm not the biggest fan of the wintertime but I do love Christmas.

As we walk up to Ellie's apartment building, I'm glad Jess even decided to wear an ugly sweater to stay in theme.

Hers is simple with a drunk Santa Claus on the front, and she's wearing a red hat to match. My sweater is a little more thought out. Upon first glance, it looks like a normal sweater, but when I raise my arms over my head it looks like a wreath.

"I don't know if this is such a good idea." Jess groans as we step up to the door.

"Why?" I frown.

"I don't know, I'm just not in much of a party mood." She sighs.

"Well maybe this will change that," I suggest with a smile.

"I guess," she grumbles but I knock on the door anyway, and Ellie greets us with a big smile.

Her pink hair is tied up to show off her ugly sweater, which is a reindeer complete with a 3D ring toss on its antlers. It's honestly adorable and fits her personality so well.

"Hi! I'm so glad you made it!" Ellie gives me a hug and pushes us inside and away from the cold. We met each other at work, and this is the first time I've been to her apartment.

"This is my best friend, Jess." I introduce her to Ellie.

"Hi! So great to meet you." Ellie greets her with a hug and Jess looks surprised but takes it with grace.

"So...the food is in the dining room, and the people are in the living room. There are kids upstairs so I'd like to keep the cursing to a minimum, but honestly, their parents are the chilliest, so no worries if you forget," she adds with a laugh.

"Sounds great." I smile and drag Jess into the living room. I'm more of a social butterfly than she is so I know she's going to want to hide out by the food even though we ate before coming. I grab her the mixed drink I promised her and a vodka soda for me, although I'm drinking more for the taste than the need. Then, I drag Jess to the living room by the hand and look for a familiar face but I don't see any. I do what I'm best at and start introducing myself to people.

"Hey, I'm Emma. How do you know Ellie?" I ask a brunette who's sitting next to an even older brunette holding hands in between them.

"We've been best friends for years," the younger one says. "How about you?"

"I work with her." I smile.

"Oh you must work in fashion then. Are you a designer?"

"I am," I say proudly. It's taken years to get to this position, and I wear it proudly.

"I'm just this one's girlfriend. So I've only known Ellie for a few months." The older one interjects with a hand extended.

"I'm this one's plus one. I don't know anyone here," Jess says lightly, and we all laugh.

"You'll get acquainted quickly. Everyone here is mostly gay and very open to inviting new people into the fold," the older one says.

"I'm Bella by the way, and my girlfriend is Dylan. How long have you two been together?" she asks innocently.

"Oh, we're not together." I brush her off quickly. We're used to people mistaking us for a couple because of how close we are and the fact that we're both openly into women.

"Oh, my mistake." Bella blushes.

"She's just my best friend," Jess adds with a smile.

"That's amazing," they say. We make small talk about Ellie and what they do for work. Bella is currently unemployed but Dylan runs a publishing company with the blonde woman, Lucy, across the room. She's standing next to her very pregnant brunette wife, Morgan.

"Oh! You've met my bestie and her girl! I have more people for you to meet, mind if I steal her for a few?" Ellie asks Jess, who looks anxious but I know she's going to say it's okay. She wouldn't tell Ellie that she doesn't want to do something.

"No worries." Jess forces a smile, and I mouth a quick apology. I don't know who Ellie wants to introduce me to, but I want to get acquainted to as many people as possible. I'm still new-ish to the design industry, and Ellie has been doing this for almost five years now. She can introduce me to names and people that I otherwise wouldn't even know of.

"So, a few of my model friends are here, and I thought you'd want to meet them," she says with a smile.

"I'd love to." I smile.

"Hey girlies, this is the designer I was telling you about. She does clothing from size oo to 6XL+, and she's looking for some models. I thought you guys might want to be acquainted," Ellie says proudly.

It's true, just as Ellie believes in bridging the gap for plus-size clothing and being able to have cute clothing in all sizes, I believe the same. But unlike Ellie, I make my clothes available in all sizes. Just changing a few things from the smaller sizes to the bigger sizes to better fit those with bellies and rolls. I'm always looking for new plus-size models to showcase my designs for my portfolio. This is something Ellie knows, so I'm sure her introductions are very intentional.

"I'm Gia." A blonde extends her hand with a smile.

"I'm Charity," another blonde says.

"I'm Kenzie," a brunette says as she smiles.

"It's so nice to meet you guys, do you have cards or anything I can take home with me?"

"We do! We never go to an Ellie party without one. Kenzie laughs.

"Ellie loves to pimp us out," Gia adds.

They each hand me a card with their info and over walks a very pregnant blonde. Are all the blondes here pregnant? I'm going to need to catch up or something. Not that I'm in any rush to have a baby, I'm only twenty-six, but one day it'll be nice.

"Hey, baby, they didn't have the beer you like so I made you a mixed drink." the blonde says, smiling with pink lips. She's dressed in an oversized pink sweater that has a circle carved out to look like a snow globe where her belly is. It's incredibly creative and cute.

"I love your sweater." I smile.

"Thanks! I actually made it myself," she says proudly. "I'm Barbie. I don't think we've met."

"Barbie? Like the doll?" I ask, surprised.

"That's the one," she says, laughing. "My parents are toymakers, so I think that had something to do with it."

"It's very cute." I smile. "I'm Emma, my parents are boring." I shrug.

"I like the name Emma, we might have to add that to our list, huh babe?" She looks at Kenzie as she grins.

"It's definitely cute," Kenzie agrees.

"Hey!" Jess comes over interrupting the conversation, politely.

"Guys, this is my best friend Jess. Jess, this is everyone," I introduce her.

"Hey everyone." She smiles politely.

"What do you do Jess?" Kenzie asks. I wince, hoping no

one would remind her that she's unemployed, but it was a simple question.

"I'm actually between jobs right now, but I was a librarian," she says.

"Oh, that's awesome. I'm sorry to hear you're between gigs right now. I'm a model, so I know too much about that," Kenzie adds and the rest of the girls nod in agreement.

"It's a tough world right now," Jess says with a shrug.

"That it is."

"I should go check on the food—and Reese. I think she's still playing with the kids upstairs," Ellie says shaking her head.

"We have some people to say hello to, but you should definitely give us a ring if you need models; we'd be happy to work for a friend of Ellie's," Charity says.

"Of course." I'm glad we came to the party. Knowing more models will help my career.

"Can we go yet?" Jess asks quietly when everyone walks away.

I pull her to the side, under a doorway so we're not in anyone's earshot. "Why do you want to leave?"

"Everyone just keeps asking about my job, and I have to be reminded over and over that I'm unemployed." She sighs.

"I'm sorry. I guess you can leave if you want to, but I really want to stay. I'm having fun."

"Okay—" Jess is cut off by the sound of everyone chanting.

"Kiss! Kiss! Kiss!" It takes me a moment to realize that Jess and I are standing under mistletoe. How ironic. We both smile and shake our heads but the chanting doesn't stop.

"It's bad luck if you don't kiss!" someone shouts.

"Come on! You gotta!"

"Just go for it!" another person says.

"Fuck it," I mumble and before I know it, my hands are on Jess's face, and I'm pulling her toward me for a kiss. Our lips press against each other's under the mistletoe and the chanting becomes silent behind us. It's almost as if the entire world stops the moment our lips touch, and I feel something I've never felt before.

Oh shit.

Chapter 5

Jess

The second Emma's hands are on my face, I'm too shocked to move. In what feels like a millisecond, her lips are pressed to mine, and I have to take a second to breathe. I kiss Emma back with all I've got. I give her everything, and I don't think twice about who she is and the fact that we most *definitely* shouldn't be kissing right now. No, I'm kissing Emma back with my tongue slipping into her mouth and hers slipping into mine, our kiss deepens until we both pull back.

"Whoa," I mumble quietly, but Emma looks at me with a friendly smile. She looks completely unfazed, like she didn't just basically make out with me. Like our tongues weren't in each other's mouths half a second ago.

The crowd goes back to talking amongst themselves, and I look at Emma, unsure what to think. That was one of the best kisses I've ever had in my life, and she looks completely normal—like that kiss was just a normal thing to her. Is it possible she didn't feel the same? I mean, what am I even feeling? It isn't like I suddenly have feelings for my best friend, but fuck if that kiss didn't awaken something in me. Suddenly, Emma isn't just *Emma* anymore; she's this beautiful woman I kissed and felt fireworks with. Is it because we're so close? Such good friends? I'd never kissed her before, but I had to believe that was what it was. I mean, it can't be anything more than that, right?

"You want to get home right?" Emma narrows her eyes at me.

"I-I'll actually stay," I stutter out. I don't want her to know I'm staying in hopes that we might kiss again.

"Oh! Okay, then I think we should make you some friends," she says, smiling. She takes me by the hand like she's done a thousand times before, but this time I feel a jolt of electricity shoot through my veins. It's like every nerve in my body sparks to life.

"I don't want to make new friends, why don't you socialize and I'll be around," I suggest.

"Are you sure?" She looks at me with an eyebrow raised.

"I'm positive." I smile. In truth, I need a moment to take in everything and figure out what the hell is going on with me.

"Okay. Come find me if you need me." She lets go of my hand, and I notice how the loss of her touch makes me feel. It's like I've suddenly become addicted to the touch of my best friend, and losing it is too much.

"Okay." I nod and head to the kitchen to find myself a second drink. I need more alcohol, and I need to think more clearly. Yes, I'm aware of how contradictory those two things are. But I need a drink to clear my mind first, then I'll focus on clearing out this brain fog.

I help myself to a vodka with a splash of cranberry juice and a maraschino cherry. I take two hearty gulps, and the room becomes a little fuzzy; it's been awhile since I last ate, and I might've made the drink more vodka heavy than I should've. In my defense, I'm at a party with no one I know, and I just kissed my best friend for the first time. I mean... we've been friends since middle school and never once has anything romantic happened between us. I always thought we were meant to be best friends until we died. But now I'm seeing her in this whole new light, and I don't know what to do about it.

How could one stupid mistletoe kiss change everything? And is it just me? I look over at Emma, and she's smiling to herself while talking to a new group of people across the room. She's in her element, clearly not uncomfortable in the slightest. How could she just kiss me and not say a second word about it? Is she really so immune to me? I know Emma is more of a hookup type, but is that how she saw our kiss? It's just another one to her, nothing special?

I make myself a third drink, and this one goes straight to my bladder. I walk around the brownstone in search of a bathroom. When I finally find it, there's a lesbian couple making out in it, so I close the door quickly and they come out a moment later with their heads down in embarrassment. I'm in no place to judge. I got drunk because my best friend kissed me, and I have no idea what all of this means.

I pee, sitting on the bowl for far too long as I think about that kiss. I'm in the kind of drunken haze that makes me a bit fuzzy. My stomach is in knots, but not in the throwing up kind of way. At least I have that going for me. I wash my hands and set off to find my best friend. I need to see if there are any signs of her mentally freaking out as much as I am about this kiss. I mean, if she is too, then maybe the two of us can just talk about it and laugh it off. By tomorrow morning I'll be back to normal, right? It's probably the vodka, the fact that I haven't kissed anyone in a bit, and the fact that it was Emma. I mean, that has to be it, right?

"Hey, bestie." I smile, walking over to Emma and Ellie.

"Hey, I see someone found themself a drink." Emma chuckles. *Has her laugh always been that cute?*

"I did, maybe three," I slur just a bit.

"Oh gosh." Emma and Ellie laugh.

"So what are we talking about?" I ask.

"Emma, you were telling me about that hookup with the cutie from the mailroom at work. Are you going to see her again?"

I feel a twinge of jealousy as I hear Ellie asking her about another hookup. I don't know why. I mean, Emma is notorious for hooking up, and I'm used to her stories about who she hooks up with. It's nothing new, but this jealous feeling definitely is.

"Oh, I don't know. I think she's looking for something more casual."

"You're not?" Ellie asks.

"I don't know what I'm looking for, but...I think I want something more serious right now." Emma pauses to look at me. Was that some sort of hint? Or am I drunkenly reading into things? I shouldn't have had that last drink.

"I get that. Although, when I met Reese, I wasn't looking for anything serious and she surprised me," Ellie says with a romantic smile.

"Are you going to hookup or go out with that girl who asked you out tonight?" Ellie asks after a moment.

"What girl?" I can't help myself or how jealous I sound. The words slip from my mouth without a second thought.

"Oh, a girl from the party tonight asked her out. She's super-hot." Ellie smirks. "Don't tell Reese I said that." She laughs.

"I don't know," Emma says shyly. What's up with her?

She's never shy about these kinds of things. I knew far too much detail of her last several hookups.

"Who is she?" I ask looking around the room.

"The blonde with the sweater that looks like a Christmas tree," Ellie points out.

Fuck. She *is* cute. Why isn't Emma jumping at the chance to hook up with her tonight? Or in the future. That girl is definitely her type, so why isn't she going for it? Could it be because of our kiss? I don't want to get my hopes up. What the hell is going on with me tonight? Am I really this bent out of shape over one kiss with my best friend?

"She's cute," I say quietly, and I notice Emma clench her jaw.

"She's more your type than mine, honestly." Emma shrugs.

"You're both into women? I love that. You must be incredible wing women to each other knowing the other so well," Ellie says, practically gushing.

"We are. When we go to the bar, we have a good line that usually works." Emma laughs.

"Oh god, it's from a television show. It's not even our own line."

"What show?" Ellie raises an eyebrow.

"*How I Met Your Mother.*" I crack a smile. It's true—when Emma and I are together, we're like Ted and Barney being able to pick up any woman and take her home easily. Of course, it's mostly Emma taking women home and me taking them on dates. I'm more of a serial relationship person than a one-night stand kind of person.

"I've never seen it, but now I'm curious."

"Trust me, it's not that great." Emma shrugs it off.

"It's my favorite show," I say with a scoff.

"No, I meant our move. It's not even original," Emma teases.

"Oh." I should've realized she wasn't insulting my favorite show.

"You okay? You look a little pale." Emma looks at me as Ellie walks away to talk to someone else.

"I'm okay." I look at her, confused. I don't feel pale. If anything, I feel hotter than usual.

I want to bring up the kiss but this doesn't feel like the time or place. I don't want to bring it up because I don't want to ruin our friendship in any way. Not that it's so fragile that we can't talk about a kiss, but I don't want her thinking it means more to me than it means to her. She looks calm, cool, and collected, and I'm over here drunk off my ass about it. It's so stupid. We're friends, I should just stop overthinking it and call it a night. I need some food and water, honestly.

"Are you ready to head home?" Emma asks.

"Are you?" I ask. It's already after one a.m., but I've never known of her to leave a party so early. She's usually one of the last to leave.

"Yeah, I have work to do tomorrow."

"But it's a Sunday," I point out.

"Yes, but my boss wants it ready by Monday, so I need to work a bit tomorrow. I'm going to call us an Uber; I don't want you walking home and falling on your drunk ass," she teases.

"Fine," I grumble, knowing she's right. I'm always a bit clumsy when drunk.

"Let me go say goodbye to Ellie." She looks at me. "Stay here."

"Yes ma'am." I salute her, and she rolls her eyes with a smile.

I stand in the corner and watch her cross the room with ease. Not like me, someone with social anxiety. She gives Ellie a hug goodbye, and I know I shouldn't be jealous, they're only friends. They are way more platonic than the two of us. But still, the thought of Emma being with anyone else right now is enough to make me jealous. She's so beautiful, her blonde hair is covered in cute little red ornaments that are clipped in to make her hair look like a tree. It's so creative and original, and I love how beautiful she looks with them. She has minimal makeup. She looks so good with little to no makeup on—or no makeup on at all. I think about all the times I've seen her barefaced and in pajamas, and she's just as beautiful. Is it possible I missed it all these years? That someone so beautiful could be standing right in front of me? I mean, it isn't like I'm blind to her beauty, but I always thought that meant I wanted to be her, not be *with* her.

Chapter 6

Emma

I'm expecting Jess to be hungover as hell the morning after the ugly sweater Christmas party. I mean, she was downing those drinks like there was no tomorrow, and she's always been a bit of a lightweight. I made her favorite breakfast to cheer her up. Eggs scrambled with crispy bacon and orange juice with no pulp. I'm just waiting for her to wake up. The food is sitting in the microwave and ready to be heated up. I've always been an early riser; it's something I'm used to from getting up for work so early every day. Meanwhile, Jess is more of a late sleeper. She's always a little late to work because she loves those extra five minutes of sleep. To me, once my alarm sounds, it doesn't make a difference—I'm awake. I decide to take her dog, Duke, and my dog, Ivory, for a quick walk around the block to let them both go potty. I was happy when she moved in because at least Duke and Ivory get along and like to play together.

But what's really on my mind is how Jess and I kissed last night. I tried to play it off like it was no big deal, but inside, I've been freaking out. It doesn't help that the person

I usually freak out to is now the person I'm doing the freaking out about. I don't know what I was thinking. But everyone was shouting *kiss, kiss, kiss*, and I just decided to go for it. I mean, I thought it was going to be an innocent kiss between friends, not some big deal. Then again, it wasn't like Jess and I had ever kissed before. So I really shouldn't have known what to expect. In reality, it was just a kiss. But to me, it was also something more. I'd never felt that strong of a reaction from *just* a kiss before. It was like our lips were made for each other's. I wanted to kiss her again and again, but I knew I couldn't. I didn't want to ruin our friendship. Especially over some stupid mistletoe kiss.

"Good morning," Jess says, walking out of her room. She's still dressed in the pajamas I gave her last night, and I feel like a creep for noticing this, but she's definitely not wearing a bra. Not that she usually does. Her breasts are small enough to get away with not wearing one—but still.

"Morning, I made you breakfast," I finally speak. Why is it suddenly so difficult to talk to my best friend. What the hell is wrong with me?

"Ooh thank you. I'm so freaking hungover. I had way too much to drink last night." She groans as she makes herself a fresh cup of coffee.

"You did," I tease.

"Well, if there are free drinks, I'm there." She shrugs. She acts like she's such a partier when I literally had to drag her ass out of the house last night.

"Oh, yeah." I roll my eyes.

As she reaches in the cabinet for a mug, I hear her gasp and I know what she's seeing. I spent the morning adding her mugs to my cabinets so she could feel a little more at home. I know they are some of her favorite things in the world, and she deserves to have them accessible in her cabinets.

"Did you do this?" She smiles so big and looks at me.

"I did. I just wanted you to feel like this is your place too."

"Well now it definitely does." She smiles and grabs a mug from the cabinet. I'm too far away to see exactly which one she takes.

"Oh, I'm so excited to drink this coffee now," she mutters to herself. And I'm so glad I woke up and thought about doing that today.

I'm watching Jess move about the kitchen, doing her own thing, and I'm wondering if she's always been this beautiful. Like, I know she didn't magically get hotter overnight, but how did I never notice how beautiful my best friend is? It feels like I'm overthinking this kiss. I mean, one kiss can't possibly be having this much of an effect on me, can it? I mean, it was a good fucking kiss, but was it the best kiss I'd ever had?

Yeah. that's exactly what it was.

It was one of the best kisses I'd ever had. Her tongue slipped in my mouth so gracefully, and I can still feel the way her lips felt on mine. Subconsciously, I touch my lips with one finger, as if I can feel the sensation of her kiss one more time.

"Did you eat?" Jess asks, sitting down on the couch across from me. Oh my god, if she even knew what the hell I'm thinking right now.

"Yup, I'm on my coffee now." I like to eat first and have coffee second, while Jess is the opposite. She loves having her coffee first and then eating.

"Are you doing anything today?"

"Nope, today's my lazy day. I might draw later, but that's just for fun." I smile.

"I have to do some job hunting, I think." She sighs. I know it's been bothering her so much that she's been putting it off.

"I can help if you need." I offer.

"Thanks, but I think I got it."

"Okay." I nod.

We sit in silence for a bit. It's a comfortable silence, though. When we're together, we just enjoy each other's company without the pressure of speaking all the time. So, I sip my coffee while she drinks hers, and I try not to think of her in the ways I have been. I mean...she's my best friend for fuck's sake. But as I look at her lips as she takes a drink, I can't help but notice how plump and noticeably kissable they are. It isn't like her beauty is a new thing to me, it's just that I'm suddenly seeing her completely different. Almost like that kiss awakened something deep inside me. And I can't do a damn thing about it.

I wonder—silently—if she feels the same or if she's just normal after our kiss. She's been acting a bit weird lately, but she had just been dumped and kicked out and fired; I don't know what normal is for her right now. I just feel weird bringing it up like it means something to me because what if it didn't mean anything to her? Then I'll make everything weird between us—and that's the last thing I want. She needs some normalcy and stability right now with everything going on. I can't say *hey kissing you felt nice, wanna do it again?*

But then again, it was the first time I'd ever felt sparks fly with another person. Am I just supposed to ignore that and go back to kissing strangers? No. That's the last thing on my mind, which feels out of character for me. I don't want just anyone right now. I want to explore what I'm feeling for Jess.

"You look deep in thought," Jess muses, breaking my inner thoughts.

"Oh, nah." I shrug. I can't very well tell her what I'm so deep in thought about.

"Thinking about that girl you're seeing?" she asks.

"What? No!" I answer a little too quickly—and a little too harshly.

"Oh, I thought maybe you were thinking about calling the girl from the party."

"Nah. I don't think I'm going to pursue that." I pause. "Do you think I should?" I know it's lame, but I'm searching for anything from her.

"It's up to you," she says with a shrug. I hate how nonchalant she's being. But that's how she usually is about my dating life, and I mean, how do I expect her to react?

"Are you thinking about dating again?" I ask curiously.

"Me? Ha! That's a good one." She laughs and I frown at her.

"What's the joke?" I ask.

"I just had my life and heart stomped on. What the hell do I have to offer anyone else right now?" She scoffs.

I hate how much of a pessimist Jess could be when it comes to, well...everything. She's always so much more negative than she needs to be.

"You have a lot to offer as a person. You're an amazing human," I remind her with a soft smile.

"Thanks, but you're my best friend you have to say that."

"That's not true. I'd be honest if you sucked," I tease.

"Would you?" She raises an eyebrow.

"I would."

Jess stays silent, like she isn't sure what to say next, and honestly, I'm not sure either. I'm basically trying to convince my best friend, who I might have feelings for, to go out and date someone new. What the hell is wrong with me? Am I really be okay with her dating and, god forbid, coming home with someone? The thought puts knots in my stomach, and I don't know what to think. I have no right to stop her from being happy or being with anyone else, but on the other hand, here I am thinking about her in a whole new light.

I decide to get my mind off things and change the subject. What could we talk about that's friendly and nonromantic territory? I think about a few different topics, but everything comes back to the kiss we shared. I'm obsessing a bit, and I need to clear my head. Damn that stupid ugly sweater Christmas party. Oh! Christmas! I can as her what she's planning on doing for Christmas. We haven't talked about it yet, and I'm curious about it. I mean, is she staying here? Seeing family? Obviously, she isn't spending it with Camille anymore.

"What are you doing for Christmas this year?" I ask, smiling. I already have a whole day of things planned for the holiday season, and I want to get Jess as involved as possible.

"Uh, nothing." She scoffs.

"Wait, what?"

"Em, I just got dumped and fired. I'm not celebrating shit this year," she retorts.

"But it's Christmas time," I point out, frowning.

"So?" She looks at me like I'm the crazy one.

"Wait, are you saying you don't like Christmas?" I ask.

"I mean I'm not *not* saying that." She shrugs and looks at her coffee.

"Jessica Grace."

"Oh god, don't middle name me." Her eyes widen and a panic look spreads across her face.

"You cannot sit here and tell me you've basically lost the holiday spirit and expect me not to do a thing about it!" I exclaim.

"I do, actually."

"Well, you should know me better than that."

Jess sighs.

"Look, I know things are tough for you, but it's the perfect time of year to change that. We can turn things around the holiday way." I smile.

"I don't know...." She hesitates.

"Well, what *do* you know?"

"That I don't feel very Christmassy right now. Let alone have any holiday spirit."

"Pass me my iPad. I need to take care of this," I say.

"Oh gosh." She sighs but reluctantly hands me the iPad.

I open it and decide to draw a brief list in Procreate. I've always enjoyed drawing better than writing, and I know my handwriting is fancy enough. So, I start thinking of Christmas and holiday things for us to do together. I look up the Rockefeller tree lighting, but apparently we missed the actual lighting of it by a few days. So I Google and look on Pinterest for cute ideas. Jess is next to me the whole time, not paying attention to what I'm doing. She stands to grab her breakfast and eats it in its entirety before I'm finished. Then I think the curiosity gets the best of her.

"Okay, what are you doing?" she finally asks.

"I'm making a list of things for us to do this holiday season." I smile.

"How many things are on this list?"

"Twelve." I smile proudly in true holiday fashion.

"So what's number one?" She sighs.

Chapter 7

Jess

"You don't have to come job hunting with me," I insist.

"You don't have to come Christmas shopping with me either, but it's way more fun to do things with your best friend," Emma points out.

"Okay," I groan out.

We walk along the snowy streets of New York City. The slush under my boots is slippery as we step in black-covered snow puddles. It isn't beautiful like the tourist photos of New York imply—it's actually disgusting this time of year. The snow turns black the moment it falls, and the sludge is a mess to walk through. It's too wet to be called snow but too thick to be called anything else. I hate this time of year for many reasons, but this is my main fight. I trudge through, following behind Emma who seems to be perfectly fine ignoring it. It seems to be a trend lately.

She was perfectly fine ignoring the kiss. Not that I want to talk about the kiss either. Well, I do. But I don't want to be the one to bring it up. Especially when she acted so normal afterward. I mean, it doesn't seem like it bothered her or affected her in the slightest. Not that I'm looking for some big reaction, but it's been a week now and she's yet to bring it up even casually. I thought we might talk about it when we were alone, but it seems like the plan is just to forget it ever happened. I just wish it was as easy for me to forget about it as it is for her.

"Come on!" Emma grabs me by the hand and tugs me out of the way just at the last second. A car wooshes by and sprays the sidewalk instead of me.

"Shit. Thank you," I mumble. A second later and I would've been completely covered by the sludge I was just complaining about. Not exactly the look you want to go for when you're dropping off resumes for potential jobs.

"No worries." She smiles and I look down, realizing we're still holding hands. Both are gloved, but I swear I can feel the electricity radiating from her body. Did she feel it too?

"Oh, sorry." She fumbles and lets my hand go suddenly. I frown at the loss of contact.

"Is this where you wanted to go?" I ask, looking up and ignoring the feelings swarming inside of me.

"Yup," she says smiling.

It's Fifth Avenue, which is basically a few blocks of stores I can't afford to shop at. But Emma has insisted on going in and at least looking at the window displays of each one. I have to admit, they are kind of cool. It isn't like I'm blind. The displays must have taken someone a long ass time to think of and put together. It makes me think of the window displays Ana and I used to put together at the library. We were in charge of the windows looking warm and inviting for the community. I wonder who's in charge of that now. It isn't like they're going to get just anyone to do it. But I guess that shouldn't be my concern anymore. I sigh.

"What do you think about this?" Emma asks, pointing up to a red Santa-themed dress. It's strapless with white fur along the top and bottom.

"It's perfect for a Christmas party." I smile. I can see Emma rocking it with her small curves and delicate figure. She looks similar to the mannequin it's hanging from.

"I was thinking of grabbing it for fun. I don't know where I'd wear it, but I love it too much not to get it," she gushes.

"You should at least try it on," I suggest.

"Okay!" She nods and we walk into the store. It's warm with our heavy winter coats on, but someone comes over right away to help Emma and I'm left to my own devices.

I aimlessly paw at the clothes on the rack. I can barely afford to breathe in here, let alone buy anything. The clothes are beautiful, but way out of my budget. Especially these days. But Emma and I are knowingly in different tax brackets. It helps that she has a good job, but it helps even more that she has family money—not that anyone else knows about that. She doesn't like to flaunt it, but her family is a big deal in our small town and she definitely came from money, unlike me. Growing up, I was lucky to get twenty dollars on my birthday from my parents. To say things were tight for them is an understatement.

"Jess! How does it look?" Emma struts down the middle of the store—not caring who's looking—with her bare feet. Fuck, she looks hot. Her breasts fill out the dress perfectly, and the rest hug her curves exactly like I imagined. The only thing missing is a Santa hat on her head.

"Jess?" She looks at me, and I realize I've yet to answer out loud.

"You look great." I clear my suddenly very dry throat.

What the hell is wrong with me? Why am I lusting over my best friend like a damn creep?

"Thanks!" She turns to the saleswoman. "I'll take it." She grins.

I watch as she heads back to the dressing room, and her perfectly round ass bounces with each step. When did I turn into an ass girl? Honestly, when did I turn into someone who thought of their best friend like this?

"Ready?" Emma smiles as she walks over with her new bag.

"Yup." I nod, swallowing lightly. I need some water or something.

"I need to grab something for my sister and my parents next," Emma says, looking at her phone as we step outside the store.

"I need to grab something for my parents too," I add. Not that I'm going to buy anything off Fifth Avenue, but the reminder is important.

"We can stop on the way home somewhere for them." She smiles.

"Okay." I nod.

We look at the lit up windows as we continue walking in the sludge. Emma walks through it casually like it's not even there, and I trudge through like it's the worst thing I've encountered all day. I have a bag full of my resume to hand out when we're done here, and I'm growing anxious about it. It isn't like any of these places said they're hiring online, but I figure it can't hurt for them to keep my resume. I'm trying to be proactive. I can't go months without having a job. I wouldn't know what to do with myself, not to mention the fact that I need the money. Sure, I'm living rent free for now. But eventually I'll want my own place, and I need to be able to pay first, last, and a deposit all on my own.

We stop at a few more stores on the way to the libraries. Emma buys a present for her parents in one of the many stores we stop in, and I'm just glad to get out of the cold—even just for a little while. Emma and I are opposites when it comes to shopping; I would much rather do my thing online, and she is definitely more of an in-person shopper. I just don't need the looks of other customers or shop workers judging what I'm buying or not buying. It's something Emma seems to be oblivious to. Or maybe she just doesn't care what other people think. How I wish I could be more like her in that way. But my anxiety doesn't allow me to do so. I care too much about what people think and how they might be judging me. It's something I work on every day, but it isn't something that'll change overnight.

"What do you think of this?" Emma asks, holding up a green blouse. It's pretty but it isn't really her style.

"I love it, but it's more me than it is you." I laugh.

"It's for you, dummy. You need a nice interviewing blouse." She smiles and rolls her eyes.

"It's nice Em, but I can't afford a new shirt right now," I say shyly.

"Think of it as a gift." She shrugs and hangs it over her arm.

"Em, you don't have to." I shake my head.

"I want to. Gift giving is my love lan—"

"Language, I know. But still, you don't always have to buy me things." I frown.

"It's how I show my love. How will you know I love you if I don't shower you in things you don't need?" She puts her hand on one hip, and I know I'm about to lose this fight.

"Okay, fine," I say with a heavy sigh.

"Yay! I'll be right back!" she exclaims and runs to the register before I can change my mind.

I smile, shaking my head at how cute she is. I know how much she loves shopping for other people, but it's adorable to see in person like this.

"Here you go!" She comes back and hands me a bag to carry.

"Thank you," I say begrudgingly.

"You're SO welcome." She smirks.

I just shake my head and we head to the next store before Emma decides she's done shopping for the day. We decide to stop at a diner nearby and eat a quick lunch. I eat my burger without onion rings so my breath is still nice and fresh for any type of meeting with people. I don't want their memory of me to be that I could've used a breath mint. I change into the new shirt, since it goes with the black pants I'm wearing. Emma insisted I change into it, and I don't want to disappoint her, plus I figure a new shirt can't hurt. I need all the help I can possibly get. We head to the New York Public Library first, and I have Emma wait outside the front office. I don't need her threatening anyone into hiring me like I know she wants to do. She can be a *very* overprotective best friend.

"Hi, can I speak to Maureen?" I smile, hoping her receptionist will let me in. I know Maureen from working at the other library; we've spoken on the phone and met in person a few times. I'm hoping she might remember me and be able to take me on.

"I'm afraid she's in a meeting. Can I ask who you are?" She lowers her glasses to look at me.

"I'm Jessica. I was hoping to speak to her about applying for a job here."

"We're not hiring," she says sternly.

"I know, but I was hoping I could just speak to—"

"We're not hiring. She's not seeing anyone about any job today or any other day." She cuts me off with a sharp tone.

"Okay. Can I just leave my resume with you then?" I ask hopefully. I go to pull one out of my bag and she stops me.

"No."

"But—"

"Look, I'm sure you're very qualified but she's not hiring and leaving that here would just give me more paperwork to shred," she snaps.

"Okay. Thanks anyway." I walk away feeling more defeated than when I walked in.

"How'd it go?" Emma asks, smiling.

"Not great, maybe this was a stupid idea."

"No. Even if you hear a no, it's still a place that you tried. Where's the next library?" she asks optimistically.

"40 Lincoln Center Plaza," I say looking at the list.

"Okay, this time just tell them you aren't taking no for an answer," Emma says and I just nod.

We end up walking around three more libraries today, and they all take my resume but assure me that they aren't hiring this time of year. At least they're nicer than the first place was. I take that as a small win.

Chapter 8

Emma

"**C**ome here girl!" I call before taking a seat on the couch. Ivory comes running, and I softly pet her as she sits in my lap.

Jess is getting ready for us to do another thing on the list: head to Bryant park and walk around during the holiday season. I know the shopping and the job hunting had the opposite effect on her, so I'm hoping this might work. I just wish she could be more open minded about things like I am. I don't want her to be so grumpy and negative all the time; it's like she doesn't realize how negative she is. But then again, she's also been through a lot lately, and she has every right to feel her feelings in any way she needs to.

"I'm ready," Jess announces as she walks into the living room. She surprises me by wearing a cute ass outfit. Her legs are covered in sheer black tights and a green skirt, and she's paired them with a tan sweater. She looks like a holiday model. Not that I'd ever tell her that. But she looks really good right now.

"Okay, are you bringing Duke?"

"Yes, lemme get his collar on." She grabs it from the hook by the door. "Come here, Duke." He comes wagging his little corgi tail, and she puts his boots and collar on him. I do the same with Ivory, and we're both ready to go.

"Do you want to walk there or take the subway?" I ask before we go. Both our dogs are small enough to obey the "dogs must be in bags or carriers" subway rule.

"We can walk. I don't think the snow is going to be that bad, and they actually shoveled the streets," she explains. I nod. It's also been quite a hot day, so maybe some of the snow has melted away.

We take the dogs in the elevator and then out the front door. I smile at the bellman, and he tips his hat at me. Jess leads the way to walk toward Bryant Park. They hold their annual shops around the ice skating rink at the park each year. They have a ton of shops, treats, and Christmas goodness. I'm trying to get Jess into the holiday spirit since she's gone all Scrooge on me. It's a slow and steady process, but I'm not the most patient kind of gal.

"Wow," I gush, looking at all the little green shops scattered around the park. I look over at Jess but she's grimacing at her feet instead of looking at the scene in front of her.

"What happened?" I ask.

"I stepped in poo, I think." She frowns and takes a seat on one of the chairs the park has. Thankfully it's not covered in snow. "Oh yes, I definitely did."

"Shit," I mumble and she looks up at me and we both laugh. I didn't mean, *shit* shit.

"Give me something to scrape it off with." She sighs and hands me the leash for Duke. Looking around, I pick up a stick, and it makes Ivory and Duke jump with excitement.

I hand the stick to Jess and then look at the dogs. "Sorry

guys. The stick isn't for you. We can't play here." They look at me like I'm speaking a different language.

"I think I got it all, and hopefully walking around will get rid of the rest." Jess grimaces. She tosses the stick in the garbage, cleanses her hands with hand sanitizer, and takes back Duke's leash.

"Did you see the shops? They're all decorated like a little Christmas village," I say with excitement.

"Oh, wow." She forces a smile and mine falls. This is going to be harder than I thought.

We decide to make a loop around the shops before going inside any of them. I'm not planning on doing too much shopping, but I could always use a stocking stuffer or two. I know Jess still has a lot more of holiday shopping to do, though, so it doesn't hurt to take a look inside the little shops. I'm a little chilly about halfway through so I insist we stop and get some hot cocoa to warm us up. Jess secretly loves hot cocoa, so I know she can't resist. They even give us a little candy cane to stick in the inside of it, and I plop it beside the marshmallows they've put in. I feel like a little kid sipping on a hot cocoa instead of a coffee, but it's a delicious holiday treat.

"How's yours?" I ask.

"Good. My candy cane was broken, though, so I didn't put it in."

"It might taste better all broken up," I suggest.

"That's true. Give me a sec." She reaches in her pocket, opens the lid of the hot cocoa, and dumps in the candy cane remnants. She takes a hearty sip and smiles. "You were right."

I love being told I'm right. We pass by a puppy store as they're giving out free treats, so we give Duke and Ivory one each and they gobble them up within seconds. Ivory is a bit of a slow walker, and with her fur styled, everyone is stopping us to ask if they can pet her—and of course I oblige. Duke isn't as friendly to strangers, so anyone who goes up to him gets a low grumble. It's funny, really. Duke is almost like a dog version of Jess. I'd never tell her that, though. They just both have similar mannerisms when it comes to dealing with the world.

"Did you want to go ice skating?" I ask, looking at Jess and staring at the ice skaters.

"So I can fall on my ass in front of a hundred people? No thank you." She laughs.

"We'd have to leave the dogs anyway," I point out.

"I do want to visit the bookstore they have here, if that's okay." Her face lights up as she asks.

"Of course!" I'm happy there's something she actually wants to do here.

We walk over to one of the bigger shops and stop at the bookstore. It has all new releases, all genres, and a section of just holiday books. Jess gets lost in the book section, and I take Duke from her and she doesn't even protest. I'm standing on the side, leaning against the column, waiting for her to finish browsing. There aren't too many people in the shop so she's able to look around a little more thoroughly than the other shops we've been to. I admire the way she picks up and holds each book with such verocity. She treats every book like a child and holds it with care. She's smiling and laughing as she reads the back of some of these books, and I wonder if I've been going about this all wrong. Maybe I need to find some way to incorporate books and reading to this holiday challenge. Maybe gifting her a book after each new holiday adventure we go on? Or something like that. I want her to be happy, and I need to find things that organically make her happy.

"I'm just going to grab this really quick." She smiles as she holds a book close to her chest. I nod and she heads to the register and pulls out her wallet. I notice the way she brushes her long dark hair from her eyes and the way her cheeks are pink from the cold. She's never looked more beautiful.

I still don't know what to do about my growing feelings for Jess. I mean, it clearly isn't going away anytime soon, and I don't know if I want them to. Maybe in showing her how to love the holidays, I can also show her how to love me, too. No. That's stupid, isn't it? We've been friends for so long because we never let anything like *feelings* get in the way of us. It's too late for us to be trying anything new. Besides, I'm fairly certain she doesn't feel the same way about me. She hasn't brought up the kiss from the party either, so maybe she doesn't think about it as much as I do.

"Ready?" I ask as she walks over to me and extends her hand for Duke's leash.

"I thought we could walk around a little more if that's okay with you? It's so nice here." She smiles.

"I'd love that." I nod.

We pause at the ice skaters again, and this time she takes them all in without making any sassy comments about falling on her ass. Ivory and Duke begin chasing each other, and as we try to stop the two of them, we end up with our legs tangled in the leashes. I'm trying to steady myself, and just before I go to fall, Jess catches me. Her hands graze the small of my back as my legs go in the air and then she's fully grabbing onto me and catching me. I look deep into her dark eyes as she looks into mine, and I swear the rest of the world stops as she holds me. I don't hear a single sound, or feel anything besides her fingers on me. I catch my breath as she helps me stand up. Our lips are so close to each other's that

I think something is about to happen. Then time begins to pass between us again, and I blush at how intense that felt. It looked like we were about to kiss but at the last second we didn't. I don't know who pulled away, if it was her or me or both of us. But I feel the tension thick in the cool air as I clench my jaw and she looks at me, waiting for me to say something. I'm speechless as she bends down and untangles Ivory and Duke.

"You okay?" she asks, looking at me.

I nod. I don't trust my voice right now.

"We should probably head home before they try to tangle us up again." She smiles.

"Okay," I agree. Did she not feel the tension that was hanging between us now? There's no way she can ignore it. It's clear as day that something is going on between us. I just don't know *what*.

She hands me Ivory's leash, and I walk next to her as she holds Duke's and the pups get along now. They're just sniffing each other and acting like nothing happened—just like Jess is doing. She's pretending things are the same as they've always been while I'm here overthinking the smallest things and wondering what would've happened if I had leaned in and kissed her. Would Jess have rejected me? Would she have let me kiss her again? Would she kiss me back? I didn't know the answer to any of these questions, and the unknown is slowly killing me.

We walk home together in the dark in silence. I don't know what to say to my best friend for the first time in our lives, and I think she's feeling the same. Or maybe she's confused about what she's feeling. I should just say something, but I don't know where her head is at and I don't want to say the wrong thing. So I don't say anything. By the time we make it home, it feels like we've walked miles, and Jess stops outside the apartment building to take clean off her shoes. She assures me I don't need to wait for her and tells me to head upstairs, which I take to mean she needs some time alone and I don't blame her. Maybe she needs a second without me or a second to clear her head, either way, I'm right there with her.

I take off Ivory's boots and then my own, and then I shrug out of my coat and head to my room. I try to think about what I want to say to Jess but nothing comes to mind. I mean, what do you say to your best friend who you secretly want to kiss?

Chapter 9

Jess

After I almost kissed Emma again last night, I try to keep my distance from her. It was a stupid, last second thing that thankfully I thought better of. The last thing I need is to do something stupid and kiss Emma when she doesn't want me to and ruin our entire friendship. Some drunken mistletoe kiss is different than a sober one in the middle of the park. I push the thoughts I've been having about Emma out of my head and try to give us some distance. Last night she was already in her room by the time I got my boots cleaned off, and I was thankful to avoid another awkward encounter. I hung out in my room while she was getting ready for work, and I just left my room now after hearing her leave. I take Duke out for a quick walk in my pajamas and then head back into the apartment. It's going to be a long day of looking up places that are hiring, and I need all the energy I can get. I have an extra big cup of coffee, and I pull up my laptop on the kitchen table.

I need to broaden my horizons and see what else is out there besides being a librarian. Sure, I could use my degree for other things, right? I look at the job board and decide to apply at a few temp jobs just for the holidays because some income is better than nothing, and I can't survive off my savings for very long. Thankfully, I have my own account, but I've used a lot of my savings to move in with Camille—which was clearly a waste of time and money. But I try not to chastise myself too much for that. I know it wasn't my fault that my ex cheated on me. She has her own issues and at least I'm out of that environment and in a much better one.

"What do you think, Duke? Should I apply to be a bartender at some bar called Puzzles?" I ask him, and he shakes his head.

"I agree." I was a bartender while in college but I don't want to go backward. I want to be able to move forward.

I scroll through a bunch of book related jobs and even apply to some bookstores. None of them are ideal but at least I'd be around books. I'm looking for *better than nothing* jobs at this point. I just want to be able to give Emma some rent money and pay my way. It's the holiday season and she's insistent on going out a lot, so I want to make sure I can afford to do all the things on her list. Not that she lets me pay, or that she would even show me what's on the list. But I want to be able to offer to pay if the time comes and she lets me.

Emma texts me around lunch time.

EM:
Can you meet me at Macy's after work?

ME:
Sure. Why?

EM:
#3

For a moment I'm confused—until I realize she's telling me it's the next thing on her list. I have to admit, this list isn't exactly fun so far, but it isn't terrible either. It just isn't as bad as I thought it was going to be. Unless we're working our way up to the really bad stuff. I'm not sure how I feel about it. Plus, it makes Emma happy, and lately that was all I care about. I love seeing a smile on her beautiful face. It's like she's one of Santa's elves trying to bring out the Christmas spirit in me. I doubt I have any Christmas spirit in me, but I'm still going to let her try. I just wish I knew what she had planned for us.

By the time I make it to Macy's, I see Emma's green jacket in the crowd of people and I wonder what the hell we're doing here. We've already done the whole window shopping thing. Are we doing that again? I know Macy's has some nice decorations but I'm kind of, like, immune to them. To me, once you see some displays they all seem to look alike. I don't know why I'd need to keep seeing more. I'm going to give Emma the benefit of the doubt and let her take me wherever she thinks we should go.

"Hey!" she calls out as she finally sees me. Her face lights up like I'm her favorite person, and I silently wonder if I am. I never used to care about things like that before, but now I'm just curious if I am.

"Hey, what are we doing here?" I ask after elbowing my way through the crowd of people.

"I thought we'd write a letter to Santa!" she exclaims, but I can't help but laugh out loud. It's a mistake, I realize, when I see her face drop. Fuck, she was being serious.

"Oh, you're serious."

"Yeah, I am." She frowns.

"What do you mean, exactly?"

"I mean, we're going to write down what we want from

Santa and then mail the letter to the North Pole." She holds up a piece of red paper and a white paint marker.

I lean in close and whisper in her ear, "But Santa isn't real."

"I know. But we're getting the Christmas spirit back in you, and that includes healing your inner child. You need to ask for what you really want this year, and maybe if you're good you'll get it."

"Em." I frown. She has to be joking. This may be one of the stupidest things she's ever told me to do. It feels childish as hell. What the hell is the point of doing this?

"No, you're not going to bah humbug your way out of this. You promised you'd try. So just try with me. Please." She flutters her blue eyes at me, and she must know the effect they have on me because I can feel myself giving in.

"Okay, give me the stupid marker." I groan.

She hands me one and we walk into the Macy's. It's a little less crowded inside but not by much. I find an empty wall to lean against and write down what I want while Emma does the same with her paper. I have to think about what I want to write, and I sigh, I don't ask for toys like a child would. I write down three things that I want and then I fold up the note.

"Can I see?" Emma asks.

"No." I shake my head. "Isn't it, like, if you see it then it won't come true?"

"I think that's only with wishes."

"Well, this is kind of like a wish," I point out.

"Okay. Keep your secret wishes. I won't tell you mine either then." She holds hers close to her chest.

"I need an envelope."

"I got you covered." She smiles and hands me a pre-addressed envelope.

Ugly Sweater Christmas

"Thanks." I fold up my note, drop it in the envelope, close it, and hand it to her.

"Nope, we have to drop it in the box." She points to the box, and I look at her, my brow raising.

Sure enough, there's a red mailbox sitting in the middle of the store just waiting for kids—and I guess us—to put letters in the mailbox. I feel a little stupid doing it, but I take a deep breath and walk to the mailbox and drop my letter inside. I feel a little bit better just having written something down and letting it go. I mean, it isn't like anyone will read the letter. It's all for show, after all. Still, I feel better just from dropping it in. Emma follows suit and then decides we can go back home.

"Do you feel any different?" Emma asks.

"Am I supposed to?" I ask her, confused.

"I don't know, maybe more Christmassy?"

"Sure." I shrug.

"I'll take that as a no. It's okay. There's more stuff on the list to try. But today, we have a little more to do."

"What do we have to do?"

"Come with me!" she says excitedly as we make it back to the apartment building. Instead of heading to our floor, she clicks the button for the basement and leads us to the storage unit she has.

"We have to decorate for Christmas of course," she says like it's obvious.

"Oh joy," I say with mock enthusiasm.

"Come on, you won't be saying that when Mariah Carey is blasting in the background." She smiles.

I help her grab the boxes from the storage unit and the bag she has the reusable plastic tree in. I tease her about not getting a real tree, but she says they die too quickly for it to be up and worth it. She likes having the pretend tree up for the entire holiday season. We manage to get everything up to her apartment with one trip and a paused elevator. I grab a glass of cold water and plop down on the couch. Duke runs over and jumps on my lap while Emma starts opening boxes. She tosses up her blonde curls into a high ponytail, and fuck, the back of her neck has never looked so sexy before. I have the urge to stand behind her and nibble on her ear while my hands begin roaming her body. I know it's more than just feelings that I'm having; I have a full-on crush on my best friend, but I'm also trying to keep it to myself. I don't want to do anything to let on to how I'm feeling—no matter how strong the feelings get. I'm just accepting them and moving on.

Emma puts her Bluetooth speaker on and starts blasting Christmas music from the speakers. As she opens boxes, taking out decorations and things, she begins shaking her ass. It's hard to keep my eyes off it because it's right in my line of sight, and damn...Her ass is sexy as hell. Round as a damn peach and just as squeezable. She's shaking her ass, and then I notice she's backing up right toward me. I don't say anything until she stops just a foot away from me and turns around.

"Come on! Dance with me!" she yells over the music.

I shake my head but she reaches out her hand anyway, pulling me to my feet. I don't want to dance, but I also don't mind dancing when it's with her. So I let her take the lead, and I put in the smallest amount of effort, but it turns out dancing like that actually takes more effort. So I give in and smile as I watch Emma dance wildly and crazily along to the Christmas playlist on her phone. As it goes from one song to the next, she's belting along to the lyrics, and I'm laughing to myself. For such a beautiful girl, she really does have a terrible singing voice. But I listen as my best friend belts out all the words to the song as I hum and dance along. She's putting up tinsel and garland and lots of decorations on her shelves. I watch her in awe. Is it possible to be falling even harder for someone you know you shouldn't be with? Someone you *know* you shouldn't be attracted to?

Chapter 10

Emma

Lately it feels like Jess is avoiding being alone with me. I can't tell if it's something she's doing on purpose or not, but it feels a little intentional. Like today, when I walked in the living room she suddenly had to take Duke for a walk even though he wasn't asking to go out or anything. I think there's something going on with her, and I can't tell if it's because we almost kissed the other day or what. I thought that was another harmless, almost kiss, but maybe she's scared. It was an almost kiss with her best friend, after all. Maybe I should just go ahead and talk to her about what the hell the kiss means. I want to tell her that it means nothing, but of course that would be a lie. I just hate the way she's acting around me. Maybe it's time for another thing off the Christmas list that'll force us to spend time together.

I pull out my iPad and look at the list I created; there are a few things we could do, but the thing that sticks out to me the most is getting drunk at an igloo in the city. There will be spiked eggnog and hot coco, and maybe we'll be able to relax with a few drinks in our systems. It's not like it can hurt at this point. When Jess comes back from her walk with Duke, I'll tell her we're going out tonight. Hopefully she doesn't have any issue with it.

I go to my closet and start looking for something to wear. I need it to be the perfect amount of flirty without being too obvious. So, I need something that's only a little bit slutty instead of full on. I paw through my closet for a bit and then decide on a pair of tight jeans with this low cut V-neck sweater that shows off my chest perfectly—and I pair it with a nice push up bra. I do my makeup, and by the time I've moved on to my hair I hear the door click open and Duke's paws on the floor.

"Hey! I'm in my room!" I call out, and I hear Jess walking toward my room.

"What's up? Oh you look nice! Got a hot date?" she asks.

"Yeah, you," I answer too quickly.

"W-what?" Her eyes widen and I smirk. It's too easy to mess with her.

"We're going out tonight. Go get dressed. It's another thing on the list," I explain.

"Oh, I don't know..." her voice trails as she frowns.

"Do you have plans tonight?" I ask.

"Well, no."

"Then you have no excuses. Go get your butt ready." I wave her off and she sighs but heads to her room.

Fifteen minutes later, Jess is dressed and wearing her winter coat so I can't tell what she's wearing except for a pair of jeans similar to mine. We head for the subway and grab the train a few stops to the place. We're both quiet the entire way there, so I'm excited to get there and loosen up a bit. Maybe we just need to relax a bit and talk casually until we can both open up. I just want to be able to talk to my best friend again without the awkwardness I'm feeling.

"Whoa, this place is cool," Jess says, looking around. It's an outdoor bar that has these dome-like igloos for people to sit inside and drink. I've been here once before last year on a date, and I thought it was one of the coolest places. Bringing Jess here was a no brainer.

"Right? What do you want to drink?" I ask.

"Ooh they have hot cocoa and whiskey? That's definitely what I want," she finally agrees.

"Perfect." I smile. I'm glad she's already more talkative. This is working like I hoped it would.

"What are you getting?" She puts down the menu.

"Spiked eggnog." I'm a sucker for eggnog and even more when it's spiked. Plus I know they make it really great here.

"You'll have to give me a sip, I've only had your spiked eggnog, and I'm curious how they compare."

"Oh, of course, but I think they make it much better than I do."

"Oh have you been here before?'" she asks, and I instantly feel dumb for saying anything.

"I have, about a year ago. I just remember the spiked eggnog," I lie. I don't want to go into detail about who I'm here with. Tonight is about us and getting over our weirdness.

"Gotcha." She smiles and looks around as we slide inside the igloo that's just for us.

"So how's the job hunting been?" I ask with a smile.

"Is it okay if we don't talk about that?" She shrugs out of her jacket, and I notice the low cut shirt she's wearing. She doesn't have as much in that department as I do, but her breasts are definitely on display tonight and I can't help but wonder if that's for me.

"Of course. What do you want to talk about?"

"How about we talk about how cool this place is. You should bring me to more places like this if it's on your list," she gushes.

"I'll have to double check the list." I laugh.

The sever brings us out drinks, and then we're alone again. We clink glasses and take a hearty sip of our drinks. I love the taste and take a second sip. It has a warm kick on the way down which makes me feel warm and fuzzy inside.

"So have you been avoiding me?" I ask Jess, and she almost chokes on her drink.

"What?" she asks, looking at me.

"You heard me. Have you been avoiding me?" I ask.

"No, definitely not."

"But you've been acting weird around me," I point out.

"I don't mean to." Jess sighs and I know she means it.

"Well, let's move past it then."

"Okay."

I can't keep my eyes off her chest; it's rare for Jess to wear something so revealing.

"You look beautiful tonight." I smile at her.

"I was thinking the same thing about you," she says, putting down her drink. We're both already finished so I flag down the waiter for another round.

"It's nice spending time with you," I admit.

"I swear you're in my head." She laughs.

"I just know you better than anyone else," I say quietly.

"You do." She nods.

I take a deep breath and scoot closer to Jess. We're already knee to knee in this small igloo. It's see-through and we can see the people outside of it, but I'm pretending it's just the two of us. I want to pretend it's just the two of us for a moment and see what that might feel like. She smiles as I move closer and put my arm around the back of her chair. I'm close enough where, if I wanted to, I could kiss her. But I don't want to without knowing how she'd react. I don't want to ruin our friendship over some stupid crush, and I'm not sure she feels the same way.

"You're quiet, what are you thinking about?" Jess asks.

"Work," I blurt out for some reason.

"Oh, what about it?"

"Well, Ellie and I hired a new assistant, and he's been doing a great job, so I was thinking about taking him out for drinks next week to thank him," I explain.

"I think this place might be a little too romantic," she says quietly. Does she feel what I'm feeling too? She holds my gaze for a moment, and the tension is so thick it starts to feel hotter in here. I'm about to make some kind of a move when the waiter comes back with our second round of drinks. Cockblock. Well, the female equivalent. But really, I should be thankful for him. Who knows what the hell I would've done?

We both drink and stay quiet as I think about what I want to say next. I think I just have to take the next step and talk about the kiss we shared. I'm a little tipsy but not too drunk, so it doesn't sound like a terrible idea. I just need to know how she feels about it. I mean, I can't keep guessing what's going on in her mind.

"Come here. You have something in your hair," Jess says suddenly. Her hand is in my blonde curls, taking out whatever she's found, and I catch my breath as she brushes her thumb across my cheek as she does it. Fuck, why does something like that have such a strong effect on me?

"D-Did you get it?" I stumble over my own words.

"Yeah, I think it was a fuzz from your sweater." She gives my breasts a once over and a smirk, and I know I've made the right decision to wear this. I mean, Jess is a boob woman after all.

I lean in just a bit closer, and I can smell Jess' perfume. The perfect mix of peppermint and something sweet—is that chocolate? No, something more seasonal though. It's intoxicating taking in all of her; it reminds me of the night we kissed. Our lips fell against each other's and our tongues slipped in effortlessly. I'm drunk off the idea of kissing her again. She's addicting and I've spent weeks craving her.

"Do you ever think about the ugly sweater Christmas party?" I ask boldly.

"Umm, what about it?" Jess asks innocently.

"Have you thought about the fact that we kissed and never talked about it?" I ask, finally. There's no more skirting around it now.

Jess looks at me with wide eyes, and I swear she almost chokes on her drink again. I wait for her to collect herself but she doesn't speak. Instead, her cheeks turn a bright red and her eyes avoid eye contact with me for as long as possible. Is she hoping I'll just drop it? I don't know how I possibly could now that I've gone ahead and brought it up.

"It's all I think about," she says quietly.

"What?" I look at her confused. That was the last thing I expected to come out of her mouth.

"It's all I've been thinking about for weeks, Em."

"Why didn't you say anything?" I ask.

"Why didn't you?"

"Touché."

"I didn't know if you had a second thought about it." She sighs.

"Of course I did." How could she think that I wouldn't think twice about kissing her?

We're interrupted by the waiter coming in and offering

us another round. We politely decline and ask for the check, which I fully intend on paying. I'm the one who asked Jess out, so it's only polite for me to pay. I want to go back to talking about the kiss but she brings up how we should probably be getting home to let out Ivory and Duke. I take the hint; she doesn't want to talk about the kiss anymore. Even though I'm still not sure where the hell she stands on it.

When we stand, I realize how drunk I am and the alcohol hits me harder than when I was sitting down. I wonder if it does the same to Jess. She looks a little glassy-eyed but otherwise normal. She's walking much straighter than I am.

We take the subway home, and on the train, there are no seats so we hold onto the pole in the middle of the car. Well, Jess does. I hate touching that pole never knowing who or what had touched it last. So I stand with my feet spread apart and try to balance myself but that proves more difficult than normal in my drunken state. The train turns and I fall right into Jess. Her body is pressed against mine, and I look deep into her eyes. She smiles for the first time and I smile back; hers is so fucking beautiful. I wish she smiled more often.

Instead of speaking, I close the distance between us and I lean in for a kiss. Pretending there's no one else on this subway, I let my lips press against hers and my tongue slip into her mouth. Hers slips back into mine, and our tongues dance together. It actually feels like we're alone until we come to an abrupt stop, pushing us apart. We both blush profusely and avoid eye contact. But I've never felt better because now I know Jess wanted me to kiss her.

Chapter 11

Jess

As Emma's lips leave mine, I feel torn once again at what I'm supposed to be feeling and what I *am* feeling. On the one hand, I loved kissing her, and my crush has never felt more validated. But on the other hand, I still don't know what it means. Does she like me or is she just having fun when kissing me? I don't want to be just another notch on her belt if that's the case.

I steady Emma with my hands, holding onto her hips while we wait for our stop. She gazes up into my eyes with a drunken smile, and I realize just how drunk she is. We drank the same amount but she's always been a light weight when it comes to drinking.

"Let's get you home," I say, taking her hand in mine as we exit the train. I don't want to lose her in the crowd. I ignore how nice it feels to be holding her hand, because this is as platonic as it comes.

"Okay," she says bubbly. I'm a little bit tipsy, but nowhere near as drunk as Emma is.

We get to the apartment and I walk her to the elevator. We ride in silence to the top floor. She's humming to herself in true drunk Emma fashion. If I listen closely I'll probably be able to make out which Taylor Swift song it is.

"Come on," I tell her as we find her apartment. I take the key from her purse and unlock the front door. I put my arm under hers and help her walk into the apartment. She isn't so drunk where she needs my help, but I don't like the way her balance is. She could definitely use a bit of help.

I carry her to her room, taking off both her shoes and helping her out of her clothes. Thankfully, she helps me and makes it easier on me. I tug off her jeans and her sweater, turning around as she looks for her pajamas. It's not like I've never seen her in her underwear before, but this feels different. After she's kissed me on the train, this just feels more intimate.

"I'm dressed!" she slurs with a cheer.

"Great," I mumble and help her into the bed. She doesn't complain, and I head to the bathroom to get a quick makeup wipe. By the time I get back, she's passed out so I carefully remove all her makeup and then head to the kitchen. I get a mug full of water and the bottle of Tylenol and place them on her nightstand. She's going to thank me in the morning for that one.

I decide to take Duke and Ivory for a walk. While I'm walking them around the block, I overthink about what happened tonight. I didn't expect for Emma to kiss me but it's not like it meant anything. She was just drunk, and I was there. It's as simple as that, so I shouldn't put any deep thought into how she's feeling. I'll have to tell her that I'm not comfortable with her kissing me when she's drunk. Obviously without telling her the real reason why.

I'm falling too hard for my best friend. I can't imagine her kissing me one more time without it meaning anything.

It's like having a taste of what I want while being told no. It's absolute torture.

I put the dogs to bed and head to my room, grabbing some clothes, and then I decide to take a shower. I needed to wash the night away. I hate that I had so much fun with her and yet we're both on completely different pages. I shampoo my hair and think about how when we kissed she ran her fingers through it. Then I close my eyes, and I can actually feel her lips on mine. Her tongue slowly slipping inside my mouth to dance with my own hesitant tongue. It was different than when we kissed the first time; there was more to it. But maybe that was just because of my feelings for her this time.

Washing the rest of my body, I convince myself that Emma and I will never be together in the way that I want. So I try to turn off my feelings for her. Obviously it's to no avail, but at least I know where I'm standing in regard to my feelings for her. I need to work on getting over her. And that's the last thing I think of before I fall asleep.

When I wake in the morning, it's no surprise it's before Emma. She's probably sleeping off her hangover like she usually likes to do. I know I need to talk to her so I decide to make us both breakfast once I hear her stirring. She goes to the bathroom, and I make some pancakes for the two of us. I add some fresh bacon for her and brew two cups of hot coffee. I make everything just the way she likes it.

"You made breakfast?!" she exclaims.

"Yup, your favorite; chocolate chip pancakes." I smile and hand her a plate.

Oh give me!" She holds out her hands and takes a seat at the island to eat.

"How are you feeling?" I ask, sipping my coffee leaning against the counter.

"Thankful that someone gave me water and Tylenol or I'd be dying. I can't believe I got so drunk." Emma sighs into her pancakes.

"I also took off your makeup for you. I hope that was okay."

"Of course! I wondered if I had enough energy to do it but it makes more sense that it was you!"

"You were way too out of it," I say with a chuckle. "Do you even remember last night?"

"I remember going to the igloo place, where they must make strong drinks! Then the subway ride with you and you putting me to bed," she says, happy that she recalls everything.

"That's all you remember?" I don't want to push her about it, but I need to talk to her about that kiss.

Emma pauses for a moment, mid bite, to think about what she's missing. Then she turns bright red, and I know she's remembered the kiss.

"I'm so sorry I kissed you!" she blurts out.

Well, ouch. That was not what I was expecting her to say.

"You don't have to apologize," I mumble.

"No I do! I was so drunk, and you were tipsy. I didn't even ask. I'm so sorry." She frowns.

"It's really fine." I clench my jaw. I can't believe she remembered our kiss and she's apologizing for it.

"You're not understanding me," Emma says.

"What?"

"I'm sorry I kissed you like that, because I didn't want our first real kiss to be like that."

EMMA

Jess looks at me, shocked, like the words coming out of my mouth aren't real. I did say it out loud didn't I? I thought there was a chance she felt the same but maybe I had been misreading the signs? I thought that she felt the same, or at least somewhat close to what I'd been feeling these past few weeks.

"What do you mean?" Jess finally asks.

"I've been thinking about you in a non-friend way since the first time we kissed at the ugly sweater Christmas party," I say quietly.

"You have?" she asks, and I swear her jaw drops.

"I have." I nod.

"I like you," she finally says, and my face lights up.

"I like you too." I smile. I'm so fucking relieved that I wasn't reading the signs wrong.

Jess puts down her coffee cup and looks at me. "So what does this mean?"

"It means you can get over here and kiss me before I come over there and kiss you." I smirk.

"Oh," she mumbles.

Jess closes the distance between us but I can tell she's nervous. "I don't want this to ruin our friendship," she says quietly.

"I think our friendship is over." I laugh. "But I know what you mean. I don't want to lose you either. I wouldn't be doing this if it was just a fleeting crush," I assure her.

"You wouldn't? I don't want to be a notch on your belt. I want this to mean something."

"You mean everything to me Jess." I take her hands in mine and look up at her.

"I really like you," she mumbles.

"I really like you too, doofus." I can't help but smile ear to ear.

"Can I kiss you?" she asks.

"I've been waiting!" I tease, and she rolls her eyes.

She leans forward and runs her fingers through my hair. Her fingers stop at my cheek, and I lean into her hand and she smiles at me. I can't help but smile back in anticipation of what's about to come. She closes her eyes and leans in close. I can smell the coffee on her breath mixed with the scent of fresh toothpaste. I'm thankful I thought to brush my teeth when I woke up too. Sometimes I wait until after breakfast to do so. I close my eyes and her lips press against mine. They're soft at first, getting acquainted to mine. There's a few quick kisses and then her tongue slides its way into my mouth, and mine collides with hers. We're both tangling our tongues together, and I feel the heat rushing to my cheeks as we do.

She pulls me forward, off the chair I'm sitting on, and presses our bodies together. I can tell she's not wearing a bra, and I want to explore every inch of her, but I remind myself to pace myself. This isn't some random hookup—this is my best friend. I could kiss her for as long as I possibly want. So, I put my arms on her waist as hers go around my neck, and I enjoy how good of a kisser she is. I've been missing out on this? Our first kiss was nothing compared to this one. I can feel every nerve ending in my body exploding while the fireworks explode in my head. It's incredibly clear that I'm falling for Jess; I can't help it. Our lips were made for each other's.

"Mmm, you're good at that," I murmur as she pulls away.

"So are you." She bites down on her bottom lip shyly. "Can we move to the couch?"

"Of course." I nod. She takes me by the hand, and I sit down across from her. This time she faces me and pulls me in by the neck to kiss me fiercely. It has more passion than the last one. She's putting her all into it and I can tell.

I love kissing Jess. So that's all we do for the next few hours. Our bodies are pressed against each other's as she grabs my breasts through my shirt. I reach for hers and feel her hardened nipples through the thin cotton shirt she's wearing. I'm soaked from the kissing and touching, but I want to follow her lead. I don't want to take anything too far and scare her or move too fast. She's special and she deserves to have every stop pulled out for her. I can already imagine our first time together, and I want it to be perfect.

So we kiss and kiss until our lips are raw from the friction, and then we kiss some more with smiles and clashing lips because we can't get enough of each other. All I want to do is get lost in Jess and her touch, so that's exactly what I do. She makes me feel like I'm on top of the world, and each kiss makes my feelings for her even stronger. I can't believe I'm kissing my best friend...

I can't believe she's kissing me back.

Chapter 12

Jess

I'm kissing Emma, and Emma's kissing me back. that's the only thing that goes through my brain as we kiss for hours and hours. I've never kissed someone for so long before without being bored or moving on to sex. But the two of us are just happy kissing and being close with each other. Her body is pressed against mine, and her breasts are in my hands. Her full and shapely breasts spill out of her bra in the most perfect way. I just want to undress her and have my way with her but I'm not trying to rush anything either. I don't know where we stand; it isn't like we're two kids, and we aren't exactly virgins. But I want my first time with Emma to be thought out. Not something because of the heat of the moment. I'm more of a romantic when it comes to sex. I don't like to have it with just anyone. I need that deeper connection first. But that's something Emma and I definitely have.

I pull back first and Emma smiles.

"Are your lips tired too?" she asks with a laugh.

"Oh my gosh. They are! I didn't know that could happen. I've never kissed someone for so long," I admit.

"Same." She blushes a deep red across her light cheeks.

"I was thinking. We should talk about how far we should take this today," I say quietly.

"I'm comfortable with whatever you are." Emma smiles. "I could have you on this couch right now, or I can wait until we've been together a little longer. Whatever you want."

I blush thinking about her taking me on this couch. "I just want to be sure we're on the same page. Are you my g-girlfriend now?"

"I'd fucking hope so." She laughs and I breathe out a sigh of relief.

"Oh good."

"I just want our first time to be special, but I think anything involving us will be," she says softly. I didn't know she could be such a romantic.

"Then I'm okay with however this goes. We can check in and feel each other up—I mean out." I shake my head, and Emma lets out a loud laugh.

"I mean, I'm all for feeling each other up," she says with a wiggle of her eyebrows.

"Get over here." I shake my head and pull Emma onto my lap.

I was nervous about being with her because she clearly has more sexual experience than I do. And I don't want to disappoint in any way. Not that I think she'd be comparing me to the other women, and I know I'll be able to please her, I just want to make sure she loves it. Not that our first time is going to be perfect, but I hope it might be as close to perfect as possible.

Instead of continuing to overthink it, I grab Emma's ass, squeeze gently, and keep kissing her as she moans quietly into my mouth. This is something I never knew I needed until right now. We lie down on the couch, Emma on top, and she stops kissing me to pull back and slide her nightshirt off. She exposes her pink lace bra and her overflowing breasts. I recognize the bra from last night, but fuck, it's so hot to actually be able to look now. I'm enjoying the show when she leans down to kiss me again. Her hands paw at my small boobs, and I suck in a breath as she reaches for my waistband.

I thought she was going for my below the belt region, but she surprises me by sliding a hand up my flat stomach and playing with my nipples. They are always sensitive, something she must be picking up on by the way she's playing with them, and it feels fantastic. The sensation shoots straight into my core. The heat pooling in my legs is nearly unbearable, but I want to take in every moment of this.

"Mmm," I hum into her mouth as she plants wet kisses on my lips. Pulling away, she begins kissing my neck and nibbling on my earlobe. It's something that should not be as hot as it is.

"I can't wait for you to fuck me," she whispers in my ear. I can feel her warm breath hit me, and I want to get her naked this second and fulfill her wish.

"Oh fuck," I groan and she begins planting more kisses down my neck. She rolls my shirt up over my chest to expose my breasts to the air. I'm about to take her bra off when I look over and see Ivory and Duke sitting and starring at us.

"Do you, uh, want to take this to a bedroom? Just so we're not being watched?" I ask.

"What?" She looks where I'm looking and nods. "Yes, we can definitely do that."

She stands up and holds out her hand, and I fix my shirt and grab ahold of her hand. I notice how nice it feels to just be holding her hand and I make a mental note to do more of that. We walk to her bedroom and she bites her bottom lip.

"Sit, I'll be right back," she commands.

"Okay." I take a seat on the edge of the bed and wait until she returns with an arm full of candles and a box of matches.

"Do you want any help?" I ask.

"Nope." She shakes her head and begins lighting the candles all over the room. I don't know what time it is because we seem to have lost all track of that with the kissing, but the room was pretty dark. So the candles illuminate the room in a romantic feel. I like that she seems to be going for a romantic vibe. This definitely isn't just about sex with her.

"I like the candles," I say quietly when she's done.

"You do?" Her face lights up as I nod. "I just wanted something special for us."

"I love it." I smile. She stares at me for a moment, and I just soak these seconds in. The moments before I'm about to have sex with my best friend. This could be one of the best things I ever do.

"Come here," I say, patting the bed next to me.

Emma comes and sits next to me, so I place a hand on her cheek and she smiles leaning into it. "You're beautiful," I tell her.

"So are you." She smiles.

"I mean it. I feel so lucky to be with someone so beautiful."

"Come on," she groans.

"I'm serious." I stare at her until a blush creeps across her cheeks. Then I lean in and kiss her again, this time slow and sensual. I want to take in this moment and every second in between.

Emma kisses me back fiercely, as if our lives depend on it, and I kiss her back with just as much need. We fall back into the bed, and this time I climb on top of her. She's still just in a bra, so I remove my shirt in one swoop and she bites her bottom lip as she eyes my chest.

"Like what you see?" I ask, smirking.

"Oh yes," she murmurs and takes my boobs in her hands. She slides her hands down my chest and around my waist, down to my ass, and then pushes me against her body.

I slip my hands around hers and play with the clasp of her bra. Setting her breasts free, I toss the bra across the room and bend down to take a nipple in my mouth between my teeth.

"Oh fuck!" she calls out, gasping. I flick my tongue over each nipple several times until she's squirming against me. Then I place delicate kisses up her chest and down her stomach, around her belly button, and above her hip bones.

Her pajama pants are hanging pretty low, and I don't think she's wearing any panties. Meanwhile, mine are soaked to the bone. I don't know how I even still have them on, truthfully.

"Can I fuck you?" I ask quietly as I look up at her.

"Yes, please," she says excitedly.

I untangle the string from her pajama pants and slide them gradually down each leg. I was right—she isn't wearing any panties. Her bare pussy is exposed with only a tuft of blonde hair in the middle.

"I wasn't expecting this, so I didn't, uh, shave or wax," she utters.

"I didn't either. I don't care if you don't."

"I don't care."

That's all I needed to know. I dip my head toward her glistening, wet pussy and slide my tongue over her clit. She responds immediately, bucking her hips toward my face. I soak in every drop of her sweet juices, and I only want more. Fuck, how did I go this long without knowing how good she tastes? I should've done this years ago. I flatten my tongue against her core and sop up every drip of her. She pushes my head down closer to her clit, and I suck gently on her sensitive bud. Her thighs clasp around my head tightly, like earmuffs, and I flick my tongue over her clit.

"Oh, fuck. Jess, don't stop," she moans out. I can barely hear her with her thighs around me, but I make out her heavy pants.

I hum against her and she goes wild. Her hand tangles itself in my hair, and I lick harder and faster for her. I can feel her body getting closer and closer to orgasm the more I lick. I just want her to come for me. I want to know what she sounds and feels like when she lets go and explodes all over me. I slide one finger into her dripping pussy, and she screams in pleasure.

"YES!"

I curl my finger inside her, feeding off her reactions, and she is so close it must be painful. So I pump my finger in and out of her pussy while I suck on her clit, and I can feel her stomach raising with each deep breath. It's only seconds before she's screaming my name and coming all over my face. I soak up every last drop of her juices as her pussy contracts, and I give her one last lick. Her thighs go limp, letting me free, and I look at my girl that's clearly spent from her orgasm.

I lie between her thighs, resting my face on her pussy as I look up at her. "How you doing?"

"Mmm," is all she says, and I laugh. I've never seen my best friend speechless. I'm usually the quiet one.

"Don't laugh! It'll be your turn once I remember how to move my body," she teases.

"Don't move. I want some cuddles."

She rests her head on my chest, and I pull her body into mine. We're on top of the covers but we don't feel the winter chill. The heat is on, and we're both sweating from what we just did. I kiss the top of her head and she smiles. I've never felt so comfortable so soon with someone, but it makes sense. Emma isn't just anyone; she's my best friend. Sharing something like this with her is essentially a new level of our friendship. Our new relationship, if you will.

I play with her hair as we both rest for a bit. I know I need to let Emma catch her breath again. I didn't know I could actually leave someone breathless; this is a new win for me. When she recovers, she lies on top of me, looks up at me with sultry eyes, and whispers, "Your turn." And I know that I'm in for trouble with the monster I've turned her into.

Or maybe I'm lucky...

Because I think I've awakened a sex goddess that's about to devour me whole.

Chapter 13

Jess

"Come on! Can't I see you yet?" I call out from my bedroom. Emma and I have a habit of mixing up which room we sleep in and which bed we have sex in. It's fun; it's like we never know where we'll end up for the night. But tonight she had made me wait in my room, and then she told me she'd be back right away but has been in the bathroom for far too long.

"No! Close your eyes!" she yells back.

"Fine," I grumble and keep my eyes closed tight.

I hear the door creek open, and I want to open my eyes, but I listen to Emma and keep them closed tightly. I feel the bed move, and I assume Emma is crawling toward me. The entire thing really makes me really want to open my eyes, but I don't know what to say. I don't want to ruin the surprise either. So I wait patiently as I smell Emma's winter perfume of mixed berries—the smell is intoxicating. I inhale her scent and realize I can also smell her shampoo, which is a mix of avocados and something else.

"Okay, open," she commands.

I open my eyes, and Emma is sitting on her knees on the

edge of the bed. She's dressed in this green and red velvet lingerie set. My jaw drops as I see her in it. It accentuates all her curves as her beautiful breasts spill out of the cups that are topped with red lace. It has little bows going down the sides of the panties, and I want to rip them off her. Then my eyes notice the straps, and I realize she's wearing garters that connect to her panties. Holy fuck. I need a second to compose myself.

"Oh my god, you look amazing," I gush.

"Really?" She blushes like she didn't expect my eyes to pop out of my head.

"Um, yes. You look good enough to eat." I groan and lean forward to pull her on top of me.

"Oh!" She squeals as I pull her toward me.

Her lips find mine immediately, and our tongues follow suit. My hands roam her body and the soft velvet and lace she's wearing. I groan. It feels even better than I could've anticipated. I take her ass in my hands and push her body closer to mine. I need more of her.

"Mmm," Emma moans lightly into my mouth as I run my hands up her thighs.

"You like that baby?" I pull away to ask and she nods. I know she has a thing for when I take control in the bedroom. It's ironic, really, for how much she takes control in her daily life.

"Get on the bed and spread your legs," I command and she flops down next to me. Her blonde hair splays over the pillows and cascades down her chest. She looks like an X-rated Disney princess.

I reach for my nightstand and pull out the magic wand vibrator I like to use on myself. Tonight, I want to see how Emma looks using it while I go down on her. Her eyes light up as she sees it, and I place it on the bed next to us. Thankfully, I thought to charge it last night.

I climb on top of Emma, sliding my body between her thighs and watching as her breath hitches as my thigh touches her center. She's always so responsive to me and the little things I do; it's like we were made for each other.

"I want to taste you," I murmur against her lips. Reaching between us, I slide my hand inside her panties and my fingers are soaked instantly. I had no trouble warming her up after all.

"Yes, please." She nods.

"How bad do you want it, Em?" I smirk, taking full advantage of how bad she wants to be fucked right now.

"So fucking bad," she mutters.

"I don't hear you asking me, though." I run my fingers up the inside of her panties and she gasps.

"I-I want you. So, so, so, bad," she stammers, out and I smile. I love having my girl writhing under my control like this.

"Good girl," I praise her and her eyes light up. Does my girl have a little praise kink? I mean, who wouldn't want to hear they're a good girl?

I decide to grab her breasts, slipping my fingers under the lace and velvet to play with her nipples. Keeping them exposed, I take one in my mouth and the other between my fingers. She moans quietly for me, and I can feel her heat on my thigh. Sucking in my breath, I move slowly down her body until I'm face to face with her panties. I don't pull them off like she clearly wants me to, but instead, I decide to tease her.

I grab the magic wand, turn it on, and ignore her confused looks. Instead, I place it over where her clit is and rub slow circles across her panty-covered pussy.

"Oh," she gasps loudly under my touch.

"Feel good?" I murmur, moving the wand around meticulously.

"It would feel better if my panties were off." She whimpers.

"In time, baby girl." I smirk. Then I put the wand down, shutting it off for a moment as I push her panties to the side. I could easily take them off but there's something hotter about doing it this way.

I dip my head down for a taste of her. A long, languid lick of her pussy has my eyes rolling to the back of my head. I can't believe how fucking good she tastes. Then, I pick up the wand again and press it to her clit. She gasps and bucks her hips toward me as she feels the light vibration on her body. She's not anywhere close to how turned on I want her to be, but I'm having too much fun teasing her. And from the wet spot on her panties, I know it's working for her too.

"Get on your knees," I command. She looks confused but listens to me. I decide to take off her panties to give me a better view. I slide them down her legs slowly, and she kicks them to the side.

"I want to know, baby girl, have you been a good girl this year or have you been naughty?"

"I-I've been naughty." She whimpers.

"Oh baby girl, then I think you need to be punished. What do you think?"

"Punish me!" she calls out and I smirk. It's too easy to take control with her.

I slide my hand up her thighs and across her ass, stopping when I get to the right cheek. Then I lift my hand lightly and slap her ass playfully. It's not enough to leave a mark, and I doubt it even hurt because I want to ease her into it.

"Come on, that was nothing." She moans.

"Okay, but you asked for it." I slide my hand up her pussy, then back to her backside. Raising my hand more this time, I hit her ass hard enough to leave a handprint and she moans out for me. So I do it again.

"Oh yeah baby girl? You like being punished?" I goad her.

"Yes! Oh, yes!" She's dripping sweetness down her thighs with every slap; I can tell this is what she wants.

"I want you to be a good girl for me," I say quietly.

"Anything." She moans.

I lift my hand and slap her ass again, this time I bend down and spit just above her ass. I watch as it drips down her tight hole and she whimpers out under me. I slap her ass once more before taking my tongue and sliding it across her ass. I begin eating her ass like there's no tomorrow, burying my face in her ass, and she whimpers out my name for me. I've always been a little more into ass play than others, and I'm so glad Emma is eating this up. I want to give her an orgasm in every way I possibly can.

I run my fingers through her dripping wet pussy and slide two of them inside her. Hooking my fingers, I pump them in and out of her sweetness as I continue eating her ass. She's moaning and writhing under my touch, and I know it's doing more than something for her.

"Oh fuck!" She's screaming into the pillows, her face completely muffled.

"I want you to come for me baby girl," I command.

"Oh!" she calls out, and I assume that's her way of saying yes. So I don't let up, playing with her ass and her pussy at the same time. I want to enjoy every second of this.

Twirling my tongue in circles, I feel her tightening around my fingers. It's like one reaction fuels on the other. So, I continue both and watch as my girl comes undone for me. Her body is shivering and shaking as my fingers are pushed from her pussy. She squirts for me, her whole body going limp as she lets out a huge gush of her sweetness.

"Holy shit." Emma falls into the bed, moving over to make room for me and collapsing on the pillows.

"I'll be right back." I excuse myself to brush my teeth and wash my face so I can kiss her. I love eating ass, but I also want to be safe about it.

"Mmm," Emma moans when she sees me again.

"What? I'm still all dressed." I laugh.

"So? My girlfriend is hot naked or not." She takes her finger and points to me playfully with a come hither look.

"You want more?" My eyes widen.

"No, I want you." She smiles.

I lean down to kiss her, and our lips melt together as one. She smiles against my teeth as she realizes what I went to do, but she kisses me nonetheless. She pulls me on top of her, and I fall into the bed, almost into her. My leg is in the wet spot she created, and I have a feeling we'll be sleeping in her bed tonight.

"Sit on my face," she demands.

"Hold on," I mumble as I stand, getting undressed for her. Sliding out of my T-shirt and boxer shorts, I toss them aside and she smiles, looking over my body with hunger.

"God you're beautiful." She smiles.

"Oh, stop." I've never been able to take a compliment.

"I'm serious. I just want to take you forever and not let go," she mumbles.

"Well, you have me."

"Get on top," she commands again, and I'm loving this side of her.

Emma slides down on the pillows, and I climb on top of her body and position myself over her face. She pulls me down so all my weight is on her face. I don't have a second to think twice about it, though, because her tongue is on my pussy and I'm in heaven. When a woman eats pussy as well as this, you have to wife her up before someone else does. Am I really thinking about something like that while Emma eats my pussy? Yes, yes I am. But I don't care; it only feels natural going this way. It's like Emma and I were always meant to be together, and I just didn't see it until now.

"Fuck me with your tongue or I'll have to do it myself," I say sternly while looking down into Emma's eyes. They widen with lust and then suddenly her tongue has a life of its own again.

I'm moving my hips at hyper speed to keep up with her tongue, and I reach down to touch my clit. Rubbing slowly across it, I begin to feel my orgasm rising.

"Don't stop!" I call out and that only fuels Emma on more. She moves her mouth even more, and I'm instantly coming all over her face.

"Oh, fuck! Oh, fuck! Oh, fuck! Emma..." I moan out as I come. I can feel her smiling beneath me, and it takes me a second to get off her face and lie down next to her.

Chapter 14

Emma

"I thought you were joking when you said we're taking the dogs to see Santa," Jess says, her tone only with a hint of sarcasm.

"Nope." I smile. I heard the place where we took Ivory to get groomed is having a special Santa event next door. They rented out the space for the day and are giving out discounted grooming for the dogs so they'll look great for a picture with Santa.

"I can't believe this is a real thing." Jess deadpans.

"Come on, it's fun!" I exclaim.

"Okay." Jess gives me a look so I decide to try something.

"Fake it for me and you won't have to fake it later," I whisper in her ear, watching as her eyes widen.

"Well, what are we waiting for, let's get these dogs ready!" she exclaims. And I can't help but laugh, maybe all she needed was a bit of motivation.

We take the dogs to the little seats the salon has for them and watch as they trim and fluff up Ivory complete with a little red bow in her hair. They do the same to Duke until Jess reminds them that he's a boy and promptly takes the bow out. She rolls her eyes and makes a comment, but I remind her to be nice so she fixes her face and sighs.

Jess is looking eerily at the Santa, and I can tell she's not a fan of men dressing up like Santa so I'm glad I nixed the idea for us to wait in line to see him. Although, I hope she's not against me dressing up like Santa, because I have a fun and sexy idea for us to do later. And it involves me dressing up in Santa lingerie. Maybe it'll get her in the holiday spirit.

"After this, I thought we'd go to the Barnes and Noble next door. I know that one's your favorite." I smile.

"Really?" Her face lights up and I nod.

"I can't wait." She kisses my cheek, and I smile, glad I had thought of it. It wasn't exactly on the Christmas list, but if it made my girlfriend smile, we were going to go.

Ivory and Duke take pictures with Santa, which are polaroids that I'm going to frame when we get home. We take them next door but Barnes and Noble has a strict no dogs rule so we tie their leashes up outside and head inside together. I hold my girl's hand, and she's smiling as she walks inside.

"Go crazy. I want to buy you a book or two." I smile.

"Really?" I watch her eyes widen.

"Of course. I just want to see that smile on your face," I admit.

"Thank you, baby." She presses her lips to mine, and I smile. I can't believe how good it feels to be with her.

I watch as Jess looks over the tables of books. She passes from the bestsellers to the romances to the psychological thrillers and back again. She touches the covers, holds some of the books, and reads the backs of them before placing them down. She does this repeatedly and then soon she has a handful of books she wants to take home. I doubt she plans on buying them all, but she's still narrowing down her choices. I loved watching her face change in reaction to the blurbs she was reading. She's just so expressive and excited to be holding onto the books. This truly is her element; I just wished she hadn't lost her job. I'd never been able to visit her at the library, but I know how much she loved it there. It's how I feel about designing.

I love that she loves to read. I wish it was something that we could do together or something we both enjoyed. But every time I pick up a book, I fall asleep. I learned recently that it's because Jess can see the whole story like pictures in her head, and for some reason, my brain doesn't do that. It's actually more common than one would think, but it sort of ruined books for me. I stick to designing, art, and drawing. That's where my creative mind thrives.

"Did you decide which you want to get?" I walk over and ask with a smile.

"Oh no. There are three floors here, babe. I can't even narrow these down. I'm afraid we might be here for a while." She frowns. "Is that okay?"

"Of course it is. I love seeing you in your element." I kiss her cheek and take the stack of books from her.

"Thank you. Are you coming?" She walks toward the escalator and I shake my head. "I want to look down here some more," I lie.

She shrugs and heads up the escalator. Once she's out of sight, I run up to the register and check out with the stack of books she's handed me. There's only five of them, but I know she'd never let me buy her so many if she were with me. I just love being able to spoil her, and it isn't like she doesn't deserve to have something like this bringing her a smile. The cashier gives me a bag, and I head upstairs to find Jess.

Instead, I find a small Starbucks cafe, so I decide to surprise her with a holiday coffee and a snack. She must be hungry; we haven't had lunch yet. I grab us each a pumpkin muffin and a peppermint mocha coffee.

Then, I walk around the store and look for Jess. It's so quiet, with the exception of the kids area, and I'm sure Jess isn't over there. Instead I find her looking at the lesbian romances and holding another small stack of books.

"Hey." I smile.

"Hey, oooh is that for me?" Her eyes light up when she spots the coffee.

"Yes! I thought you might need a little snack." I hand her the drink and she takes a sip, groaning in enjoyment.

"Keep making those sounds and I might have to find somewhere to be alone with you." I bite my bottom lip and smirk at her.

"Em!" She squeals quietly and I laugh. I love making her blush like she is right now.

"So what are you getting?" I change the subject, looking at the books in her hand.

"I was thinking about one of these, they're written by queer authors of color. I think I should catch up on what's new in case I get my job back—or get another one. Plus, they're queer! Who wouldn't want to read them?" She laughs.

"Add them to the pile." I hold out my free arm.

"Wait, did you put down those other books I had?" Her face falls.

"Nope, I just bought them. Got this nifty bag too," I tease.

"Em! You can't buy me all these books," she exclaims.

"I already did, and I'm going to buy these because one of us needs to be caught up in what's new in queer literature." I take the books from her and start walking away.

She calls after me but I wait until I'm on the escalator to look back. She looks at me with a cross between frustrated and thankful. I look down at the books and realize one of the books I'm holding is a holiday romance. Am I actually rubbing off on her? It seems so.

"Em, I'm serious. You don't need to buy me anything else," Jess says as she finally catches up to me.

"Babe, will you just let me? Because this is the first time I've seen you smile at something—besides me—all season long. I just want to make you happy in my own way."

"Only if you're sure." She sighs.

"More than sure!" I kiss her lightly and race to the registers before she can change her mind.

I pay for the next two books and add in one of those extra cute bookmarks they have by the registers. I can't help myself when it comes to shopping, and it's not like Jess can read a whole book without stopping. So in reality, I'm just helping her. I sip my coffee as the cashier packs up my books, and then I head out with Jess. She grabs Duke and Ivory who are lying on the sidewalk waiting for us to come back.

As we walk back to the apartment, I can't help but smile. Even though it isn't the Christmas list that got Jess to smile, it was something that I got her and that was enough for me. Maybe I don't have to get her to LOVE Christmas and the holidays as much as I've been trying. Maybe I should just try to understand what makes *her* happy.

Chapter 15

Jess

I hear the door open just as I hit end on the phone call.

"Hi honey! I'm home!" Emma's sing-song voice calls out.

I'm not ready to face her just yet. She's been working so hard on trying to cheer me up and get me into the holiday spirit, and right now, I'm feeling anything but the holiday spirit.

"Jess?" she calls out again, and I can tell she's getting closer to my room.

I jump under my sheets, pull them up to my chin, and pretend to be asleep. I hear the door creak open, and Emma sighs before it clicked shut again.

I stay there, just like that, wallowing in my own pity. I really wanted the job. Hell, I wanted any of them, but this one was different. I wanted it more than even my old job. It had opportunities to move up.

After a few minutes, I hear Emma clanging around in the kitchen as she makes dinner. I slowly pull myself together and head to the kitchen just as she finishes up cooking.

"There you are, sleepyhead. I wasn't expecting you to be sleeping." Emma turns around, and her expression drops when she sees me. "What's going on?"

"What do you mean?" I feign ignorance. I looked at the mirror and I thought I looked okay before leaving my room.

"You look like you got horrible news today." She put down the pot and came up to me. "Wait, did you? Did the library call you today?"

I nod.

"No?"

Again, I nod.

"Shit, Jess. I'm sorry."

I shrug. "I'm out of options. I don't know what I'm going to do."

"You're going to keep trying. There is no rush. Plus, I've got you covered here."

"Emma, you can't keep paying for everything."

"I can and I will."

"No."

"Look, just focus on the holidays and maybe pick up the search again in January? I'm sure one of the libraries will call you then."

"Emma, I don't think you get it. Every single library said no."

"I'm sure it's just because there aren't any open positions right now."

"I wasn't exactly blaming myself."

Emma's eyes go wide. "I—I wasn't insinuating that. I just meant that there's nothing you can do about it right now, so let's just focus on being happy for the holidays."

Emma drags her index finger down my collar bone. Normally, I'd lean into her touch but something about her words makes me pull back.

"Look, it's okay for me to be upset about this. I was really looking forward to this position."

"I know. But you're letting it consume you. And if you let it, you won't have any space to find another job."

"You just don't get it, do you? It's not going to consume me. I just need some time to deal with it then move on. We can't all pretend we're happy-go-lucky all the damn time."

"I'm not happy-go-lucky all the time! Things upset me, too!"

"Funny, I didn't say I was talking about you. But hey, if the shoe fits."

"You've got to be kidding me. You're attacking me because you're upset you didn't get a job. It's not the end of the world!"

"I know that!"

"Then why won't you let it go?"

"It's killing you, isn't it?"

"That you're upset about something so trivial?"

"No, that you can't control how I handle things. You can't deal with the fact that I haven't been molded into the perfect girlfriend that you want."

"I'm not trying to control you!"

"You're sure as shit trying to change me."

"I am not!"

"Bullshit!"

"You know what, I'm not doing this anymore. Have your pity party on your own."

"Fine! Go! But just know this, it's okay to not always be okay! It's okay to show some fucking emotions and to feel shit."

EMMA

I instantly regret what I've said, and I know I should take it back but I can't.

"I think we should stay in separate rooms for the night."

"What?" Jess looks at me with angry eyes.

"Let's just sleep on it, stay in different rooms tonight, and talk in the morning." I decide.

"Whatever." She scoffs and heads to her room, slamming the door behind her.

Duke runs over to her door, tapping lightly with his nose, and a second later, she lets him in. Then she closes the door again, this time a little gentler. I don't blame her for being angry; the whole thing got out of hand. We both should've taken a step back when we were upset, but I didn't think it would escalate to something like this. I put away the dishes from dinner in the sink, leaving them to be washed in the morning, and I head to the bathroom. All I want to do is take a long, hot shower and think about what the hell I'm going to say to her in the morning. But I also just want five minutes to completely clear my head.

I hate the way it feels like our perfect little bubble has popped. I know Jess is going through a lot, and that's why I've tried to keep her focused on the holidays. I tried everything I could to make her as happy as I could.

I thought it was working, but apparently not. And it became painfully obvious when she pulled away from me earlier.

Part of me wants to stay frustrated. I want to be angry with her. She made me sound like I'm fake all the time. And after nearly two decades of friendship, that cuts deep. Has she always felt that way about me? Or is it just her anger at the situation?

I decide to think it was just her anger. I can't think of the possibility that she sees me that way. Not when I know how hopelessly in love with her I am.

So I fall asleep for the first time in weeks without my girl by my side, and I barely get a wink of sleep. It's hard to rest when I feel so restless.

I wake before Jess and take the opportunity to find a peace offering. I slip on a pair of leggings, loose T-shirt, sneakers, and my coat before heading out of the apartment.

Five stores later, I finally find what I want. The moment I saw them, I knew they were perfect. I just hope that Jess feels the same way.

I grab breakfast and coffee on my way back home, hoping Jess hadn't woke up yet.

And she hasn't because her door is still shut with Duke on the other side. I quietly let him out, taking both him and Ivory outside before coming back in and getting the gift ready for Jess.

Chapter 16

Jess

I pry my eyes open to the sun streaming through my curtains. My eyes still ache and my head is pounding. I'm about to go back to sleep when I realize Duke isn't in the room anymore.

Climbing out of bed, I toss on my robe, pull my hair up, and make my way into the kitchen. Emma is standing—well, leaning—against the counter with a coffee cup in her hand, two plates of breakfast on the island, and a coffee mug that's facing me.

As I approach, already suspicious of the fact that Emma is drinking her coffee before eating, the mug comes into focus. It isn't one I've ever seen before.

When I pick it up, Emma shifts forward, leaning on the bar so her mug is now close enough for me to see.

My mouth involuntarily cracks into a smile when I see what each of the mugs say.

Bring on the Ugly! is painted on the sides of both mugs, and they each have coordinating ugly sweaters on them.

"I'm sorry," Emma breaks the silence and everything inside me melts.

"I am too." I rush around the island and clasp my hands against her cheeks, pulling her in with a deep kiss.

She barely has a moment to set the mug down before reciprocating. Her tongue darts into my mouth, and I meet her with the same ferocity.

"I just want to be able to be real with you, like we've always been. And I guess I got in my head about having to put on a good face for you." I sigh.

"I understand, but you never have to do that for me. I just want you to be you," she replies.

Her hands roam down my body as she guides me to turn. She grips my hips and tugs, letting me know she wants me to hop onto the island bar.

I happily oblige. My robe falls open, revealing that I'm only wearing a tight tank top and panties. She moans lightly into my mouth, and everything I'm worried about fades away. I lean into her touch as she lets her hands roam all over my body. I close my eyes as our lips connect and our tongues tangle together.

"I need you," she utters.

"Mmm," I agree.

She bends down to be face to face with my pussy, and a shiver runs down my spine in anticipation. She gracefully slides my panties down my legs achingly slow, and I groan. I want her to taste me already. But soon enough, her face is pressed against my core, and I'm gasping for her. Emma's tongue traces my clit, then down my slit and through my folds. I'm getting wetter for her with every lick as she devours me.

"Oh, Emma!" I call out, and I lean back on the island for support.

"Mmm," she hums against me.

"Fuck me, baby." I moan and she reaches for my chest,

freeing my breasts through my shirt. She uses one hand to play with my nipple and the other to start fingering me. Her slender fingers sliding in and out of me makes me feel full of ecstasy.

Emma's tongue darts over my clit, and I keep my eyes shut as I feel the orgasm building. She is so fucking talented with her tongue. I can never keep my orgasms at bay, nor would I want to. I'm about to come when she curls her fingers inside me and squeezes my nipple between her fingers at the same time.

"Oh, my gosh! Don't stop!" I grab Emma by the hair and push her head even closer to my core. I don't want her to move. The orgasm crashes over me like waves until I feel calm and floaty.

"Fuck, you're so sexy when you come." Emma smiles. Her face is glistening with my juices, and I'm secretly dying to know how I taste. I hop off the counter and pull her lips into mine. Her tongue slips into my mouth hesitantly, and I can taste myself on her lips. It's hot as hell.

"Bedroom, now," I command and she nods.

Taking my hand in hers, I look at her once more. I pull her back into my arms before we head to the bedroom. Emma is beautiful, but she's also so much more than that. I still can't believe she's all mine. I push her hair from her face and take her lips for a slow, intimate kiss. My best friend is mine, all because of a stupid ugly sweater party.

Or maybe because of that wish I made in that letter to Santa...

Also by Shannon O'Connor

SEASONS OF SEASIDE SERIES

(each book can be read as a standalone)

Only for the Summer

Only for Convenience

Only for the Holidays

Only to Save You

LIGHTHOUSE LOVERS

Tour of Love

Hate to Love You

To Be Loved

ETERNAL PORT VALLEY SERIES

Unexpected Departure

Unexpected Days

STANDALONES

Electric Love

Butterflies in Paris

All's Fair in Love & Vegas

Fumbling into You

Doll Face

Poolside Love

Eras of Us

Tangled Up In You

THE HOLIDAYS WITH YOU

(each book can be read as a standalone)

I Saw Mommy Kissing the Nanny

Lucky to be Yours

The Only Reason

Ugly Sweater Christmas

POETRY

For Always

Holding on to Nothing

Say it Everyday

Midnights in a Mustang

Five More Minutes

When Lust Was Enough

Isolation

All of Me

Lost Moments

Cosmic

Goodbye Lovers

Also by S O'Connor

ONLY IN SEASIDE SERIES

(*each book can be read as a standalone*)

Only for Revenge

Only for the Baby

Only the Beginning

ETERNAL PLAYERS SERIES

The Accidental Puck

About the Author

Shannon O'Connor is a twenty-something, bisexual, self-published poet of several books and counting. She released her first novel, *Electric Love* in 2021 and is currently working on a sapphic romance novel set for summer 2022. She is often found in coffee shops, probably writing about someone she shouldn't be. She sometimes writes as S O'Connor for MF romances and as Shannon Renee for Poly romances.

Heat. Heart. & HEA's.

Check out more work & updates on:
Facebook Group: https://www.facebook.com/groups/shanssquad

Website: https://shanoconnor.com